Annie Moore

Overhead

What Harry and Nelly discovered in the heavens

Annie Moore

Overhead
What Harry and Nelly discovered in the heavens

ISBN/EAN: 9783337119935

Printed in Europe, USA, Canada, Australia, Japan

Cover: Foto ©Andreas Hilbeck / pixelio.de

More available books at **www.hansebooks.com**

The Midnight Sun.

OVERHEAD;

OR

WHAT HARRY AND NELLY DISCOVERED IN THE HEAVENS.

BY

ANNIE MOORE AND LAURA D. NICHOLS.

INTRODUCTION,

BY

LEONARD WALDO, of Harvard College Observatory.

———————

BOSTON:

D. LOTHROP AND COMPANY,

FRANKLIN ST., CORNER OF HAWLEY.

PREFACE.

Mr. Huxley, in a capital after-dinner speech on Scientific Education, says: "To begin with, let every child be instructed in those general views of the phenomena of Nature for which we have no exact English name. The nearest approximation to a name for what I mean, which we possess, is 'physical geography.' The Germans have a better, 'Erdkunde,' ('earth-knowledge,' or 'geology' in its etymological sense,) that is to say, a general knowledge of the earth, and what is on it, in it, and about it. If any one who has had experience of the ways of young children will call to mind their questions, he will find that so far as they can be put into any scientific category, they come under this head of 'Erdkunde.' The child asks: 'What is the moon, and why does it shine?' 'What is the water, and where does it run?' 'What is the wind?' 'What makes the waves in the sea?' 'Where does this animal live, and what is the use of that plant?' And, if it is not snubbed or stunted by being told not to ask foolish questions, there is no limit to the intellectual craving of a young child; nor any bounds to the slow but solid accretion of knowledge and development of the thinking faculty in this way."

To the least observant it is clear there is a change going on in the manner of the education of tne little folks. Very gradually, but very surely, the idea has gained force, that in its early years, the mind requires just as skillful training, and by just as cultured teachers as in the academy and high school. There is no

3

reason why the acquisitive energy of the child should not be used to store its mind with the first elements of knowledge regarding the why and wherefore of the flowers under foot, or the stars overhead ; but to properly interest and explain, requires an objective system of teaching, and a superior class of teaching, which, as a people, we are not yet ready to pay for in our schools.

Next to the teacher, comes the book : and there is a good field for the writers who, having the genius for pleasing the severe critics which a tenth of a century can produce, shall exert their genius in presenting, in entertaining ways, the truths of Natural Science so far as they relate to things of every-day life. The present little book is an example in point. To be sure, I think the writers have rather stolen a march on the little folks in covering up a primer of astronomy under the guise of a story, but the deception is of the same nature as we use in the Kindergarten. . We appeal to the boy's interest in what he sees about him, and while he thinks he has only pleasure of the lighter sort in the story or the game, we know that some new truth is being added to his mind, some new muscle is being called into play, he is taking another step in the analysis of cause and effect, he is steadily learning to think.

It need hardly be said that this little book is not meant for a text-book even in the most modest of the " Institutes " for which some sections of our country are so justly — we'll say — notorious. It belongs in the nursery — intermediate between Cinderella and Robinson Crusoe, and perhaps somewhat displacing Sanford and Merton and dear old Mr. Barlow, though the two former must have grey beards by this time, and doubtless Mr. Barlow lies slumbering in the shades of St. Paul's.

LEONARD WALDO.

Harvard College Observatory,
   October, 1878.

CONTENTS.

OVERHEAD.

CHAPTER I.

TO HICKORY CORNERS.

"You must take him out of school," said Doctor Bonney.

"I have tried that," said Mrs. Marlow, "and the only difference is that he reads all day in his own room."

"Take away his books, then, —

turn him out-of-doors,—and tell him to play and roam about till he is hungry;—then feed him and turn him out again."

"We've tried that too, and when his father went to look for him at night, he found him in a close, dusty machine-shop, asking all kinds of questions, making friends with the men, and black from head to foot, with experiments he had been trying. He had been there all day, and had given half his dinner to a boy who hadn't enough, he said."

"Take him into the country."

"O Doctor I wish I could, but Mr. Marlow cannot leave his office for two months yet, and I am so anxious about *his* health I dare not leave him."

The poor mother had tears in her eyes as she spoke. Dr. Bonney hated tears. He rose at once. He really pitied her, but the more his heart softened the rougher his voice and manner grew.

"Send the boy off by himself then," he growled; "turn him out to pasture like any other calf; send the girl too to keep him company, but don't let him take a single book for six months, or you lose him."

By this time the Doctor was half-way down stairs, scowling and growling ominously. Mrs. Marlow followed him. She felt as if Harry's future hung upon his words.

"Can you recommend any boarding-place, Dr.?"

"Widow Parsnips, Hickory Corners, New Hampshire, he snapped. Opening the street-door, then turning back his head, he added, " Good woman — no nonsense — good place — no books — feed him well — bread and milk — come home fat. Send him to-morrow. Good-bye."

Mrs. Marlow ran down to the gate after him, and called out, " How far away is it ?" as the Doctor gathered up the reins.

" Only sixty miles."

" Sixty miles," repeated the poor mother. " Send my two only children sixty miles, to be gone all summer, with a woman I never saw ?"

" Haven't you got any old maid aunt, or run-down cousin that 'll be glad of the chance to go too ?" And then there was nothing left but a cloud of dust; but as Mrs. Marlow returned to her basket of mending, she began to look more hopeful, and presently said aloud, " Miranda Roseberry ! the very one."

Now, Miranda Roseberry was a niece of Mr. Marlow's, about twenty-nine years old, who was a teacher in one of the public schools of the city where our story is laid. She was a cheerful, bright-faced girl, and Harry and Nelly always liked to have her come to tea. She would be sure to be glad to go into the country, for her school had just closed, and she lived in rather a dingy boarding-house in a narrow street.

" I will gladly pay all her expenses if she will only go with the children," thought Mrs. Marlow ; " she is kind and sensible, and will write to me just how they are."

The good mother's face grew brighter and brighter, and her needle flew faster and faster through Harry's socks, as she said to herself, " I will go round and see Miranda before tea."

Three days after, Cousin Miranda, Harry and Nelly took the noon train for Hickory Corners, or rather for Milligan's Crossing, which was the nearest railroad station to the Widow Parsnips' house. It was a very warm day, and little Nelly, who had never been away from home without her mother before, cried all the way from the house to the train, and when she got out of the carriage her eyes were so blinded that she missed the step, and would have fallen headlong, if a gentleman who was just entering the station had not sprung forward and caught her. Mamma and Miss Roseberry were so encumbered with shawl-straps, bags, and packages, they were quite helpless, and Harry was wholly absorbed in watching a truck full of trunks which a porter was wheeling swiftly along the platform.

" I am sure the centre of gravity is outside of the truck," he muttered. " They will come tumbling over in another minute," and then he heard a scream, and saw Nelly in the arms of a tall stranger with a bushy iron-gray moustache, and pleasant, laughing eyes.

It was only an instant. Exclamations, apologies, thanks, reproof, and

then they were all in the train. A
good many good-bye kisses, a few
promises and words of advice, tears
from Nelly, pretended indifference
from Harry, wistful, lingering looks
from Mrs. Marlow, and only smiling
nods, and hopeful words from Miss
Roseberry.

Then "all aboard," and away
puffed the train, and here was the
iron-gray moustache right in front
of them, stowing away his canvass
bag in one of the wire-racks overhead, and then helping Miss Roseberry do the same. Nelly sat with
her cousin, but Harry preferred to be
alone, and would not even turn over
the seat to be more social. He was
really quite unhappy in leaving his
mother, his school, and his books,

but he scorned to show it, and so
he stared steadily out of the window,
and never spoke till they reached
Lowell, where he asked the conductor so many questions about the
mills, and the various fabrics made
there, that the man lost his patience,
and told him if he wanted to know
anything else, he'd better get out and
spend the night there.

Harry had been perfectly polite,
and he thought it very hard he
should be so snubbed. He turned
back to his window rather sadly, and
flushed very red, when he saw Mr.
Gray Moustache laughing at him.
But when that gentleman leaned over
and said, " I can tell you all about it
if you will sit with me," he rose and
accepted his offer, and was presently

engaged in a most animated talk about looms and spindles, the use of teazles, &c., &c. Miss Roseberry who had soothed Nelly, till the tired little girl fell asleep with her head on her cousin's shoulder, now beheld Harry fully embarked on an intimacy with the kindly stranger.

"Dear me," she said to herself, "his mother charged me not to let him learn anything, and here he is finding out how to weave Bay-State shawls, carpets, and I don't know what else. What shall I do? Besides, this man may not be a suitable companion for him, though he certainly looks as nice as Uncle Marlow."

She reflected a little, then said : "Harry, don't you want a banana?"

Harry reached out his hand, and took the fruit, but never offered to stir from his new friend, and Miss Miranda who had a way of hoping for the best, resigned herself to watching the windings of the log-strewn Merrimac, beside which they were steaming along, reflecting, " I dare say he will get out at Nashua, and we shall see no more of him," but presently the conductor came again to punch the tickets, and behold the stranger's was a yellow one, marked " Milligan's Crossing," just as theirs were.

" Dear, dear," thought Miss Roseberry, " how unfortunate, but it isn't likely he will board at the Widow Parsnips'."

Just then the pop-corn man came

along, and Miss Miranda became so occupied in the delicate task of getting her purse out of her pocket without rousing Nelly, that she ceased to be anxious about Harry, and was presently nibbling at the sweet, crispy kernels, as happily as a squirrel.

With her corn and the Merrimac, and her naturally cheerful thoughts, she found the hours pass swiftly.

About five o'clock the train stopped at a little unpainted shed, perched on the edge of a high sand-bank, surrounded by dense pine woods.

"A watering station," thought Miss Miranda, but just then the conductor popped his head in, and yelled " Mil'gan's," and Harry's friend began to take down the bags, and piled the packages upon his and Harry's arms, and presently all four were standing alone on the platform of the tiny station, and the train had slipped away around the corner into the forest.

19

CHAPTER II.

AT THE WIDOW PARSNIPS'

How Miss Roseberry and the children liked their boarding place, may be learned from the following letters, which were mailed to Mrs. Marlow the next evening.

Dear Cousin Sarah :

We had a very comfortable journey, and are as nicely settled as you could wish.

Our rooms are on the second floor just as you hoped. A big front room for Nelly and me, with two south

20

windows, and one west ; — and a smaller one for Harry behind it, just across the entry, with one west and one north window. They had the feather beds on top — of course, but I soon attended to that — and the husk beds seem quite fresh and clean. Mrs. Parsnips is a bright, tidy little woman, rather too much of a talker, but I don't mind that as long as she gives us such delicious bread and milk and cream and butter and honey and wild strawberries and crispy seed-cakes as we had for tea last night.

It would have done your heart good to see Harry eat! For break-fast we had brown bread and fresh eggs and pickerel baked in cream. Did you ever hear of such a thing! The beef at dinner was rather tough, but we were all too hungry to care much for that, and Harry was so interested in talking with the Professor that he ate all I helped him to without once making a cross face as he used to at home. This Professor is the only other boarder here, and he is the gentleman that caught Nelly when she stumbled out of the carriage yesterday you know. He is from —— College, and is here on account of his eyes — which the occulist said would fail him entirely if he did not give them a whole year of rest. Mrs. Parsnips told me all about him — while she was changing the feather beds — he is a second cousin of her's — " awful clever " she says—and "a master hand for talkin' to children, 'cause he lost both of his, and their mother too, with scarlet fever — ten years ago."

And that reminds me to ask you if you think Dr. Bonney cares how much Harry learns by talking, if he doesn't study or read ; for if he *does* care — we must leave here, and that would be a pity. For my part I don't see how all that the Professor can tell him will do him any harm as long as they're out of doors all the time, and the child eats and sleeps well. I had him weighed as you told me. Just seventy-five pounds, and Nelly fifty-four. Now I am going to call them in to go to bed. Don't you worry about them one bit.

Give my love to Uncle Marlow, and write soon to your affectionate niece,

MIRANDA ROSEBERRY.

P. S. They have been out on the piazza an hour or more talking about the stars.

Dear Mother:

I like this place, and I wish you were here. We went out on the hill last night and we could see the whole of the sky. Nelly said she didn't know there were so many stars. Dr. Willoughby doesn't get mad when you ask him questions. They won't let him read because something's the matter with his eyes, but he says we can talk if we can't read. I'm glad he lives here. He's going out fishing with me some day. He says when I weigh eighty he'll take me down to the village. He knows some one that has a telescope, and we can look

at the sun he says. Give my love to
father. I remembered to hold up my
head this morning, but I can't remember it all the time there are so
many interesting things. Good-bye.
You know you said you would write
to me to-day.

Yours,

H. L. MARLOW.

Dear Mamma :

I fed the chickens this morning.
Mrs. Parsnips mixed some meal and
water. There are twelve, and they're
all yellow, and just as cunning. And
the big hens came and tried to eat up
all their breakfast, and I had to drive
them away with the spoon. And
there's Major. He's a nice brown
dog, and he won't bite ; he only

jumps up and licks your face, and if you throw a stone he runs and brings it to you. You said write what I was doing, and that is all I did, and it rains this afternoon so we can't go out, and I thought I would write to you, and please give my love to papa.

So good-bye.

Your loving

NELLY.

Meanwhile the Professor, or Dr. Willoughby, as he told the children to call him, was also trying to write a letter, but was somewhat interrupted by the conversation of the children, who were on the piazza outside his window. His letter was not important, so he amused himself by

listening, and the first thing he heard
was Nelly saying :

"Good-bye, Mr. Sun, good-bye till
you come up on the other side again
to-morrow."

"Yes, but he won't come up on the
other side again," said Harry.

"Why not?" asked Nelly.

"Because *he* stays in one place
and we go round *him*," replied
Harry.

"How do you know?" demanded
Nelly.

"The teacher told us so," answered
Harry, "and besides the Sun is so
much larger than the Earth that it
would take one million and two hundred and fifty thousand globes like
ours to make one as large as the Sun!
Now, do you suppose that a great big

shiny fellow like the Sun is going to take the trouble to go round and round this little bit of an Earth! Of course not! And when he has so many Planets and Comets and things to take care of too!"

"*How* does he take care of them?" asked Nelly.

"Why, he shines on them, and warms them, and makes the trees and flowers grow, and keeps them in their places, so they won't come tumbling down out of the sky."

"How *can* they stay up there, and why don't they come tumbling down?" asked Nelly.

"Why," replied Harry, "don't you know when you have a ball with a string tied to it, and swing it round and round, if you let go

28

the string a moment, off it will fly in a straight line?"

"Yes, I know well enough how you let your ball fly in my eye," replied Nelly.

"And didn't I say I was sorry?" asked Harry.

"Yes," admitted Nelly.

"Well, then, *that's* all right," said Harry. "And so about this ball with a string to it, your hand makes it move, and it would fly off if the string didn't pull it, and so your hand and the string work against each other, and keep it going round and round. And the teacher says all the Planets and Stars and things got a motion, ever so long ago, in the very beginning of everything, that makes them move in straight lines, and that's like your hand moving the ball you know."

"How did they get the motion?" inquired Nelly.

"I don't know," replied Harry.

"Perhaps Cousin Miranda knows," said Nelly.

"But any way," continued Harry, "the Sun has the power to pull the Planets towards himself, just as the string pulls the ball, and so they keep moving round and round in circles—no, not circles; more like ovals.

"Do you suppose it's true, Harry?" asked Nelly.

"Why, of course I do," replied Harry. "Our teacher knows all about it. Any way he says that is what they *think* is the reason. And

they call the way the Planets move
one long word, and the way the Sun
pulls them another ; but I've for-
gotten both of them."

"You mean Centripetal and Centrifugal force," said the Doctor, suddenly speaking through the closed
blinds, near Harry's ear, and making
him bound from his seat so hastily
that Nelly could not help laughing.

"I should think you were one of
those balls, and somebody had let
go the string," said she.

"O, Doctor Willoughby," said
Harry, "if you are not busy do
come out and help me tell Nelly. I
never can remember the long words."

So the Doctor came out and took
a seat between them.

"Centrifugal is a long word, Nelly,"

said he, "but it only means that power that makes anything fly off in a straight line, and Centripetal force is what keeps it from flying off by drawing it back. If Centrifugal force should be destroyed the Planets would all fall to the Sun, or if Centripetal force should cease they would fly off in straight lines."

"I'd much rather fly off in a straight line than fall into that great hot Sun," said Nelly, but sober Harry looked so shocked that she felt ashamed, and added, gravely:

"Are Planets the same as Stars?"

"The Planets belong to the Sun's family," replied the Doctor, "and the Stars are their cousins farther off. I will tell you the difference some other time."

" It was Sir Isaac Newton who found out about these forces, wasn't it ?" asked Harry.

Portrait of Newton, engraved by J. Smith.

" Yes," replied Dr. Willoughby, " more than two hundred years ago. Just think, Nelly, he was sitting in

33

his garden, and he saw an apple fall, and it set him thinking why it should fall to the ground instead of flying off to the right or the left."

" How funny!" exclaimed Nelly. "When I see an apple fall, I only wonder if it's a good one."

" Yes," said Harry, "and you run and pick it up, and take a bite to make sure."

"Course I do," said Nelly, "it's the best way to find out."

"It made no difference to Sir Isaac Newton," resumed the Doctor, "whether the apple was good or not. It was its *falling* that interested him, and he thought it over, until he came to the conclusion that the Earth has some power to draw or attract toward itself all falling bodies, like apples, or hail-stones, or leaves, or rain-drops. This power is called Attraction of Gravitation. If it were not for this power, as the Earth turns on its axis, everything would fly off, as pebbles and bits of earth fly from a carriage-wheel turning swiftly."

"O, how dreadful that would be," said Nelly.

"You needn't be afraid, Nelly," remarked Harry, "there's no danger of it."

"No, this beautiful law of attraction prevents it," said the Professor, "and Newton discovered that this power does not belong to the Earth alone, but that the Sun and the Planets all pull or attract each other, just as the Earth does the apple.

Indeed every particle in the universe attracts every other particle."

"The Sun has more power than the Planets, hasn't he?" asked Harry.

"Yes," replied the Doctor, "because he has more particles of matter. The attraction depends upon two things. The distance one body is from another, and the number of particles a body contains. The more particles a body contains, the more power it has to attract another body. The nearer two bodies are together, the more strongly they attract each other. The Sun attracts the Planets nearest to him more strongly than those which are farther away. It is so beautifully arranged that all the heavenly bodies are kept in their proper places by this same law of Gravitation, which makes the apple fall to the ground."

" I don't understand it very well," said Nelly, with a sigh ; " I thought it fell because it was ripe."

" So it does, Nelly," replied the Doctor, pulling her curls, " but when it is ripe, the stem grows dry and weak, so the apple has to come when the Earth pulls it ; while before it was ripe, the stem was strong and fresh, and held it tight to the tree."

At this moment Miss Miranda appeared in the doorway, and said :

" When the stars begin to peep,
" Little girls must go to sleep."

Nelly ran to her at once, for to tell

the truth she was getting a little tired of so much wise talk, but Harry begged for fifteen minutes more, which she granted him on account of his superior age.

Chapter III.

PLANETS VERSUS CHICKENS.

" O, see those two stars so close together!" exclaimed Nelly, as they ran out on the piazza, one clear evening. "One red and one yellow. If I was a fairy I'd jump right across."

" You couldn't, Nelly, if you were the biggest fairy that ever lived," said Harry.

"Well, I'd fly across, then," said Nelly.

"You'd have to fly millions and millions of miles," said Harry.

"O, I don't believe it," said Nelly.

39

" They look such a little bit of a way apart — not any wider than this bench."

" They are not so near each other as they look," said Professor Willoughby, who had just then joined them. " It is like the steeple and the flag-staff over there. They seem to be close together because they are nearly in a line from us, but you know the flag-staff is on this side of the river, and the church on the other."

"O, I see," said Nelly. " Well, how far off is the *red* star from us ?"

" Mars, the red star," replied the Professor, "is millions of miles away, and Saturn, the pale yellow star that looks so near it, is still farther away."

"What is that bright star shining through the elm-tree?" asked Harry.

"That is Jupiter, answered the Professor, "the largest of the planets. And there is Venus down near the sunset. See how bright and beautiful she is! She will set in a moment."

"Yes. There! she's gone!" exclaimed Harry, as Venus disappeared below the horizon.

"Do these stars all go round the Sun, as Harry says our Earth does?" inquired Nelly.

"Yes," replied the Professor, "the Planets all move round the Sun, with our Earth, like one family, and all receive light and heat from him, just as we do, and they are called Planets, from the Latin word which means to *wander*, because they seem to wander about the sky."

"Don't all the stars we see go round the Sun, too?" asked Nelly.

"No, some of them are called *fixed stars*," replied the Professor, "because they are always in the same places, and they are supposed to be suns like ours, and to shine with their own light. They seem to us to change their places because our Earth is moving by them all the time."

"Yes, I know," said Harry, "it's just the way the houses and trees fly by when you are in the cars."

"Do you believe they are really worlds like this?" asked Nelly; "Harry says they are."

"Yes, Nelly," answered the Professor, " and Mars, the red star, is supposed to be most like our Earth. With a telescope they can see two white glistening spots opposite each other, just as our polar

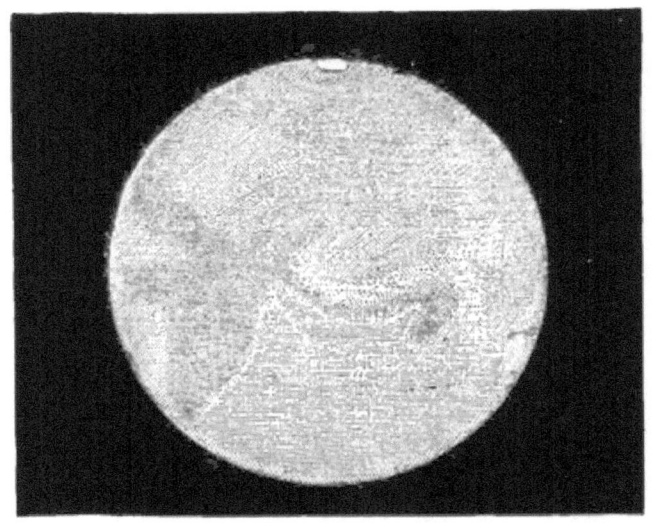

Mars, showing snow-cap at the pole, and the lands and seas.

regions covered with ice and snow might look at such a distance. Then there are bluish places which look as our oceans and seas might, and reddish portions that may be land."

"O, I wonder if anybody lives on Mars, and looks over at our Earth!" exclaimed Nelly.

"From Mars our Earth would look something as Venus does to us, very bright and shining," said the Professor.

"O, I wish we could go over there and find out all about it," sighed Nelly.

"Which is nearest the Sun, Venus or our Earth?" inquired Harry.

"Venus," replied the Professor.

"Then, is it hotter there than it is here?" asked Harry.

"Yes," answered the Professor, "and there is one Planet where it is supposed to be hotter even than upon Venus, and the Sun must look a great deal larger there too because he is

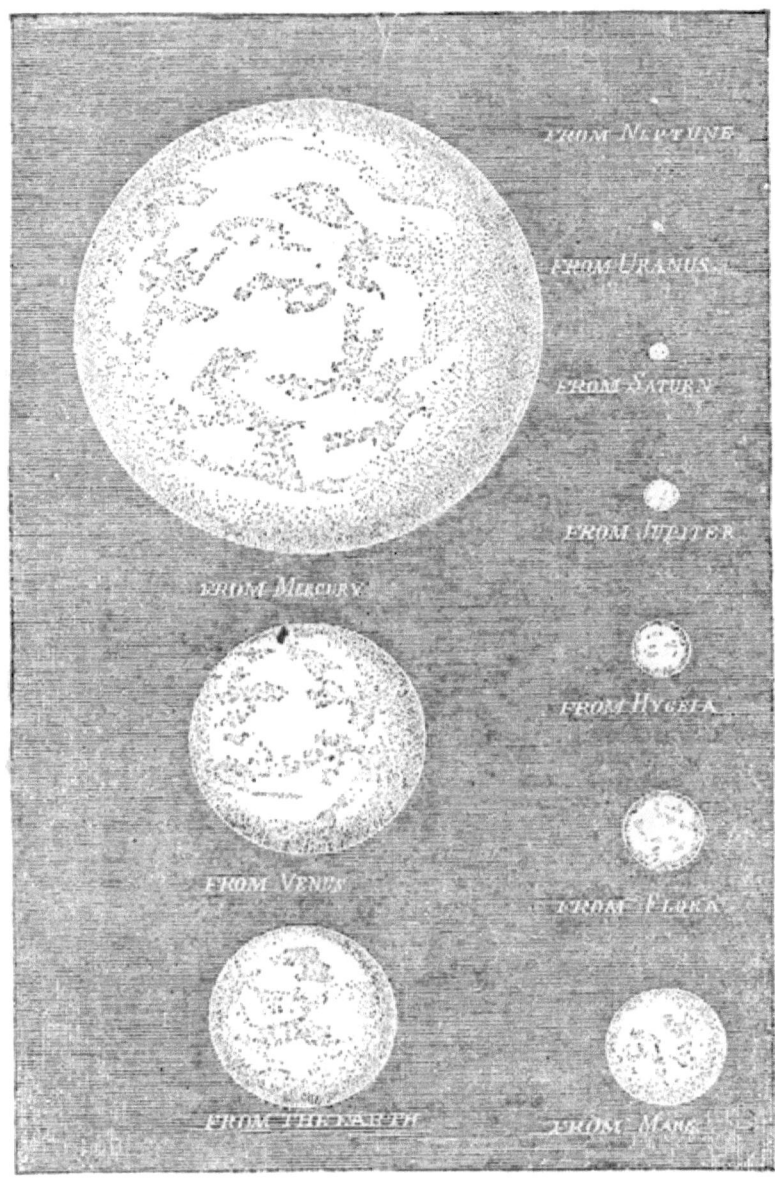

FROM NEPTUNE

FROM URANUS

FROM SATURN

FROM JUPITER

FROM MERCURY

FROM HYGEIA

FROM VENUS

FROM FLORA

FROM THE EARTH

FROM MARS

Proportional size of the Sun as seen from the different planets.

45

millions of miles nearer. It is Mercury. He is the nearest Planet to the Sun as far as we know. His path is so near the Sun, and he is so small and the Sun so bright that it is difficult to see him without a telescope.

"Did you ever see him?" asked Nelly.

"I think I saw him once," replied the Professor. "It was just after sunset, and the sky was bright and clear. I looked through my opera-glass and saw a small bright star in the brightest part of the sky. It looked almost like a spark."

"I wish I could see him," said Harry. "When I grow up I mean to be an astronomer, and have a telescope of my own."

" Perhaps you will see him then,"
replied the Professor. " The great
astronomer Copernicus never saw
him*although he often looked for

Portrait of Copernicus, engraved by J. Falck.

him ; but he had no telescope, and
Mercury can only be seen without
one in certain parts of his orbit."

* On account of the haze and fog in his latitude.

" Perhaps he was near-sighted," said Harry.

"Why didn't he have a telescope?" asked Nelly.

" He lived before they were invented," responded the Professor. " In 1609, about seventy years after he died, another great astronomer called Galileo made the first telescope."

" How did he know how to make it?" asked Harry.

" The story is," replied the Professor, "that the children of a Dutch spectacle-maker, playing with some of his glasses one day, happened to put two of them together in such a way, that in looking through them, the tower of a church near by, seemed to be brought nearer and made to look larger."

" I wish I had some to play with,"
said Nelly.

"Hush!" said Harry, but the Professor went on without seeming to
notice her.

"Galileo heard of this discovery,
and studied upon it, and tried a great
many experiments, until at last he suc-
ceeded in making a telescope which
seemed to bring the stars nearer, so
that he could see them a great deal
better."

" Did they look larger?" asked
Nelly.

"Yes," replied the Professor, "and
beside that, Galileo saw a good many
new things. One of these was that
Jupiter has four moons."

Just here Miss Roseberry came
out to look for the children.

"Only think, Cousin Miranda," said Nelly, "Doctor Willoughby says the Jupiter people have four moons. Musn't that be nice?"

"That would be just one apiece for us if we were there," said Miss Miranda, taking the chair the Doctor offered her, and drawing Nelly into her lap.

"How astonished he must have been when he first saw them," said Harry.

"He was indeed," responded the Professor. "No one had ever dreamed of such a thing before, and ignorant people would not believe that he had seen them, but insisted it was something in his telescope. Now, we have larger and more powerful telescopes, and we know that he was right in that, and in other things that people would not believe in his time."

"Does Jupiter with his four moons come next to our Earth?" asked Harry.

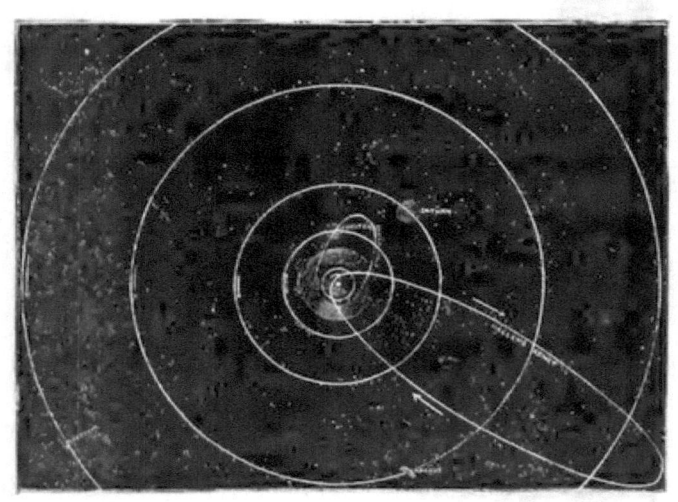

"No," replied the Professor. "Mercury is nearest the Sun, next comes Venus, then our Earth, and then Mars the red star ; then a great many smaller Planets called Asteroids, then Jupiter, with his four attendant moons, or Satellites as they are called."

"I should think," said Nelly,

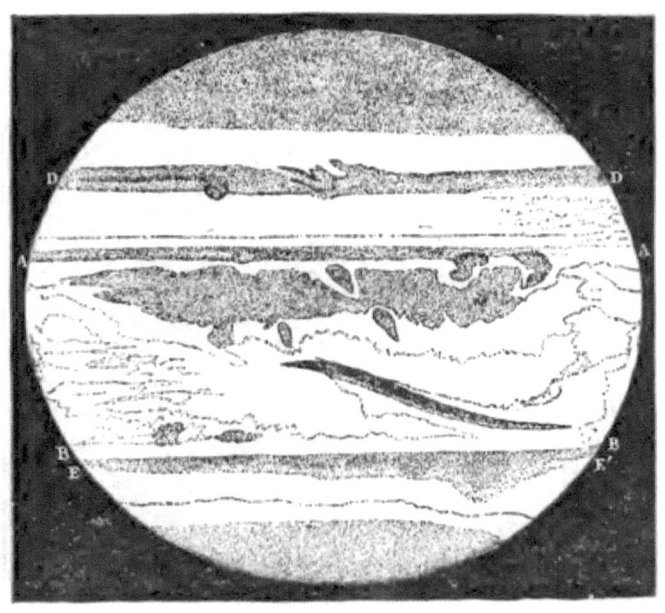

The planet Jupiter, as seen by Tacchini, at Palermo, on the night of January 28th, 1873.

"that the Sun must be something like that yellow hen we saw in the door-yard this morning, with all her little chickens running round and round her."

"And the fixed stars," said Miss Roseberry, "are like the yellow roses by the fence that do not change their places, though they are about the same size and color as the chicks."

"Ah! Miss Miranda," said the Professor, with a pleasant smile, "I see that before I finish my dull, scientific book, I must bring it to you for some poetical touches."

"And where does Saturn come?" persisted Harry, who was too practical to enjoy these wanderings from the subject in question, and who would have been an apt pupil for Mr. Gradgrind."

"Saturn's path is next outside of Jupiter's," resumed the Professor.

"He is a still more wonderful fellow, with his brilliant rings and eight moons ; and outside of him are Uranus and Neptune, who also revolve around our Sun, but are so distant from us that we cannot see them without a telescope, and even *with* one, can discover very little about them."

"Are you really going to write a book, Doctor ?" asked Harry.

"If I can only get my eyes well enough," he answered, looking so sad that Miss Roseberry hastened to change the subject by calling attention to the fire-flies, and presently Harry and Nelly were racing up and down trying to catch these "night-watchmen of Fairyland," as their cousin called them.

"How much browner and healthier your little charges look," said the Professor, turning to Miss Roseberry.

"Yes! Don't they?" she responded. "Harry does not seem at all the same boy that he was when we left Boston. I wish his mother could see him."

"I fancy he will soon be claiming my promise about the telescope," said Professor Willoughby, "but I am afraid I shall have to postpone it awhile, as my friend who owns the telescope is out of town. Do you think Harry would be content with a picnic instead until he returns?"

"I am sure he would," answered Miss Roseberry heartily. She could not help thinking how much less trying that would be for the Doctor's eyes, and how much better for the children than an evening excursion.

Chapter IV.

THE PICNIC.

THE following Tuesday Harry came running home from the village store triumphantly declaring that he had balanced eighty pounds. "And I took my knife and my compass out of my pocket too."

"Then hurra for the picnic on Thursday!" cried the Professor, who had already explained the change of plan to the children. "Run quickly and tell your cousin to be ready while I consult mine about the turn-overs and doughnuts."

Saturday morning accordingly saw

them bestowing themselves, the baskets, jugs, shawls and umbrellas in the
two-seated open wagon, which Abner
Parsnips had agreed to drive, in order
to guide them to the best road to the
summit of Hackmatack mountain.

Professor Willoughby and Harry
shared the front seat with Abner, who
was a good-natured lad of sixteen,
leaving the back seat to Miss Roseberry, Nelly, and the shawls. A little,
white-faced, long-legged colt, ambled
awkwardly after the old sorrel mare,
and Major, the brown setter, was also
in attendance.

" See, Nelly," said Miss Miranda,
"we have almost as many satellites
as Jupiter."

" How? where?" said the child,
gazing about her.

"Why, don't you see?" said Harry, "there's Sorrel, and Lightfoot, and Major already."

"O yes," interrupted Nelly; "now if Kitty Gray would only come too! O, Cousin Miranda, may I go and get her?"

"I think she would be happier at home," replied Miss Roseberry. "Kittens are not fond of traveling, and we must not leave Mrs. Parsnips all alone."

Nelly looked a little disappointed, but the last basket was now stowed away, Abner cried "Ge dab!" which was his method of starting his horse, and Nelly forgot her regrets in the excitement of waving a very small handkerchief in farewell to the widow, till they turned a corner, and were fairly out of sight of the house.

Harry meanwhile had imprudently attempted to dazzle Abner with some of his own recently acquired knowledge in regard to Jupiter's and Saturn's many moons; but as Abner only responded, "O pshaw!" he gave him up, and relapsed into offended silence.

"O dear!" said Miss Miranda, suddenly. The Professor turned towards her in concern.

"*Must* we go up this long hill, Abner?" she was asking. "I am sure it will be horribly steep on the other side."

Abner grinned, and ruthlessly replied, "O, that ain't nothin'; there's worse a-comin' when we git into Slabtown. The folks there don't know enough to keep the roads anyway decent ! " Poor Miss Roseberry looked a little pale.

The Professor felt sorry for her. She was generally so blithe, he was surprised to see that she was really frightened.

" Would it comfort you to remember," said he, " that the most rugged of these hills, is, in proportion to the rest of the Earth's surface, no more than the roughness of the peel of an orange?"

He looked at her with such evident sympathy and kindness that she could not help smiling back, but before she could reply, Nelly exclaimed, " *I* know a story about an orange! Once there was a fly standing on the top of an orange, and another fly came crawling up the side of it, and the fly at the top said, 'Aha! this orange is round!' And the other fly said, 'How do you know?' and the top fly said, 'Why, when I met you walking on the table a while ago, I could see the whole of you at once; but when you crawled up this orange I saw your head first, and then the tops of your wings, and then the rest of you; so now I know it must be round,' and the other fly said, 'I don't believe it.' So that's the way they know the world is round, because they can see the top of a ship first."

"O Nelly!" said Harry, "that isn't the way to tell it!"

"Yes, it is," said Nelly, "for I've seen a picture of an orange with

63

two flies on it in our teacher's book."

"I suppose you know all the ways to tell that the Earth is round, don't you, Doctor?" asked Harry.

"I believe I do, Harry," replied Dr. Willoughby, "unless you have

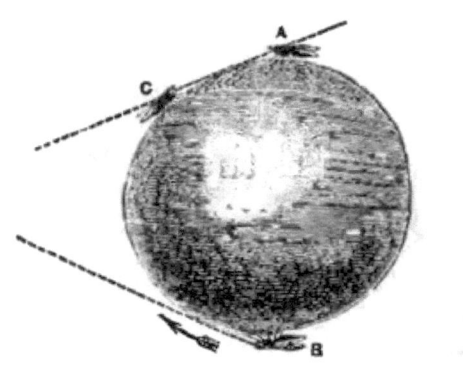

discovered some new way." Abner grinned, Harry turned his back upon him, and replied with some spirit:

"You know I couldn't!" Then recovering himself, he added: "but

I remember two ways our teacher told us: one is, if you travel right along in the same direction, you will come back to the place you started from; and the other way is, that

Phenomena produced by the sphericity of the earth.

when a ship sails from you the hull goes out of sight first, and by and by the masts, just as if she was going down hill, and when she is sailing towards you, you see the top of the mast first, and the hull afterwards, as though she was climbing up hill."

" That's just what I told you," cried Nelly.

" I think the prettiest way to prove it," said Miss Roseberry, " is by the round shadow the Earth casts upon the Moon in an eclipse. You know, Nelly, the Earth could not cast a round shadow, in every position, as it does, if it were not round itself. Look at the shadow of your head in the road now." Nelly had just taken off her hat for a moment.

" Yes," said the Professor, pleased that Miss Roseberry was forgetting her fears, " and see what a straight shadow those bars make. That is the sort of shadow the Earth would

cast, if it were flat, as in early times
every one believed; and they thought
that if you only went far enough, you
would come to the edge, and fall
off."

"Why, that's just what I thought!"
said Nelly.

"Doctor Willoughby," said Harry,
"how is it about eclipses? Does the
Earth come in between the Sun and
the Moon?"

"Yes," replied the Professor, "the
Earth and the Moon have no light
of their own, but look bright because
the Sun shines on them; and sometimes as they go round the Sun, the
Earth comes between the Sun and
the Moon, and cuts off all the Sun's
light, and throws a dark shadow on
the Moon. But the Moon is not

wholly darkened, our atmosphere re-
flects light enough to give her a dull
red color.   If she passes through the
centre of the Earth's shadow, she is

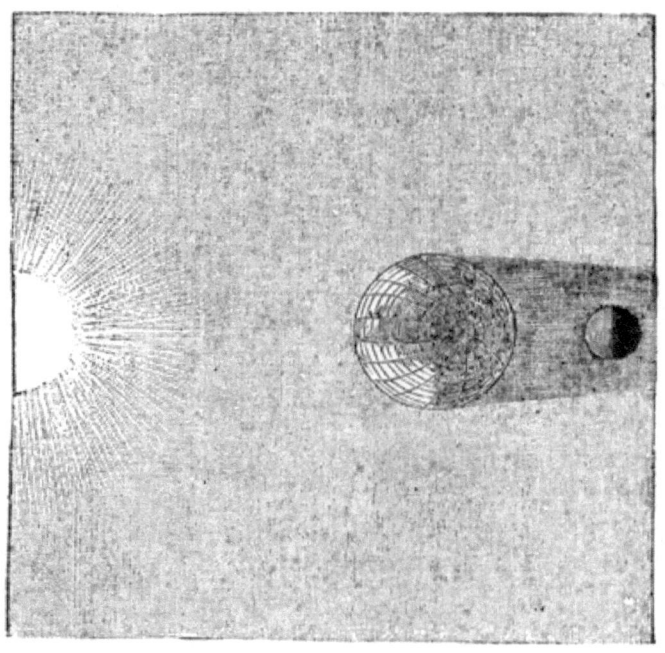

Eclipse of the Moon.

hidden nearly two hours.   Wise men
can tell exactly when these eclipses
will take place, and you can always
find a list of them in the almanac."

68

" And when there is an eclipse of the Sun, does the *Moon* come in between the Earth and the Sun?" asked Harry.

" Yes," replied the Professor, " the

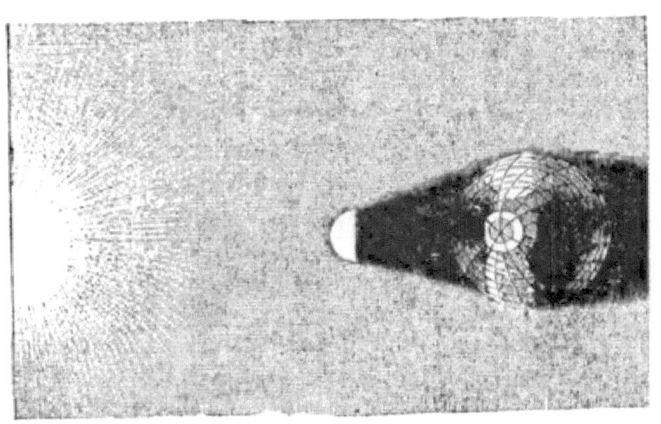

Eclipse of the Sun.

Moon is much smaller than the Sun you know, but she is so much nearer to us, that when she is in the right place, she can hide the Sun entirely ; and then the sky becomes so dark that the Planets and some of the brighter Stars can be plainly seen. This seldom occurs however.

" When the Moon covers only one side of the Sun, the eclipse is said to be partial."

" I remember seeing an annular eclipse once," said Miss Roseberry, " and how beautiful it was."

" What is that ? " asked Harry, looking at the Professor, who accordingly replied :

" That is when the Moon comes between us and the Sun in such a way as to cover the middle, and leave a bright ring all round the edge like a border of gold, and as *annulus* is the Latin for ring, it is called an annular eclipse."

" Is it the Moon's coming in between, that makes it dark at night?" inquired Nelly.

"Why, no!" said Harry, glad of a chance to administer another dose of his superior knowledge to the reluctant and unappreciative Abner. "The Earth keeps turning round like a top, and when one side is turned towards the Sun it is day there because the Sun shines on it; but when that side is turned away from the Sun it is night, because it is in the shade."

"Isn't it more like a ball with a knitting-needle run through it than it is like a top?" said Miss Roseberry.

"Yes," said the Professor. "Your knitting-needle is a good illustration of that axis we are obliged to imagine the Earth turning upon in order to understand the daily change from darkness to light."

Here Abner stopped by the wayside watering-trough to let the horse drink, and of course the children as well as Major and the colt found that they were thirsty too ; so Miss Roseberry took Nelly's silver mug out of the basket under the seat, and the Professor kindly offered to go up-stream a little way and fill it. When he returned, he presented Miss Miranda with an oak leaf full of wild strawberries, which pleased her as much as the water did Nelly.

When all had drank, and Abner had made friends with Harry by allowing him to climb down on the shaft and replace the check-rein,

much to Miss Roseberry's secret ter-
ror, they went on ; the awkward gam-
bols of the colt giving them many
amusing illustrations of partial eclipse
as he darted first to one, and then to
the other side of the road, in front of
his much-enduring mother.

" He will certainly get run over!"
said Miss Roseberry, as he blundered
against the wheel for the tenth time
in as many minutes.

" I never heerd of a case," said
Abner, with such philosophic calm-
ness, that Miss Roseberry dismissed
her anxiety, wisely reflecting that if
the owner of the colt were not un-
easy, she ought not to be. The road
now became so steep and stony,
that the Professor and Harry got out
of the wagon to lighten the load, and

before long Miss Roseberry and
Nelly decided to do the same; the
former moved by her fears of an
upset, the latter by the attractions
of wayside berries and flowers, and
her usual desire to imitate her
brother.

They all supposed they should
presently resume their seats, but
somehow they found the change of
position so restful, the breeze so refreshing, the winding road so alluring, that they straggled happily
on, now chatting, now silent, now
altogether, now singly, and then in
couples, sitting to rest on a fallen
tree, while the Professor cut canes
for them all in the alder thicket,
drinking from the brook that sang
along beside them, in leaf cups of his

twisting, Harry and Nelly loading
themselves with specimens of moss,
oddly streaked pebbles, wild roses,
and bunch-berry flowers, which they
gladly flung into the wagon whenever
it overtook them, till at last to their
surprise and pleasure the grass-grown
track they had followed ended suddenly in a ledge of bald granite, and
two minutes of scrambling carried
them to the summit of old Hackmatack. It was now twelve o'clock,
and even the wide beauty of the view
spread before them could not long
divert the children's minds from the
luncheon baskets, so while Abner
unharnessed and fed Sorrel, Miss
Miranda selected a flat rock shaded
by a grove of wind-twisted spruces,
and the Professor and Harry brought

thither the ample stores of eatables
and drinkables which Mrs. Parsnips
had provided in generous style. O!
how good the cold coffee tasted, and
surely there never was anything better than the thick slices of bread and
butter and honey, unless it might be
the mince turnovers with goodly slabs
of cream cheese ; the widow, unlike
many city housekeepers, considering
that form of pie as appropriate in
June as in January. Abner bash-
fully conveyed his share to a remote
nook in the rocks, where Harry by
and by discovered him sound asleep,
his hat over his face, and a score
of ants running unheeded over him,
busily appropriating the crumbs of
ginger-bread and pie-crust with which
he was sprinkled.

CHAPTER V.

GOOD-BYE TO THE MOUNTAIN.

" DON'T you think Doctor Willoughby was very kind to choose the longest day in the year for our picnic, Harry?" said Miss Roseberry during dinner, as she helped him to jelly.

" It doesn't seem very long to me," said Nelly.

" Is it really longer than all the rest?" said Harry. " And why is it?"

" It is the 21st of June," replied Miss Roseberry; " don't you know that in the summer we have long days and short nights, and in the winter short days and long nights?"

" O, yes!" said Harry; " I know in winter we have to light the gas before tea, and now it's light till nearly bed-time."

" Very good," said his cousin; "that shows that you have noticed that summer days are much longer than winter ones, and now you can remember that the 21st of June is the very longest of all, and that after to-day it will be dark a little bit earlier every night until nearly Christmas-time. But the difference is so very slight you will not notice it for some weeks to come. The shortest day and the longest night come the 21st of December."

" I don't know anything about long

nights," said Harry; "they always seem short to me, except when I have the toothache."

"I think the night before Christmas is *very* long," said Nelly.

"You know, Harry, how many times we always wake up before it is light enough to see what we have got in our stockings."

"Very true, Nelly," remarked the Professor gravely, as he removed the shell from a hard-boiled egg.

"But you haven't told me yet *why* the days are so long in summer," persisted Harry.

"The knitting-needle through the ball that your cousin told you of, would help you understand that," said the Doctor; "perhaps this egg and my pencil will do as well. The

egg is the Earth, the pencil is its
imaginary axis, and this glass of jelly
will do for the Sun. If the axis were
upright," said he, holding the pencil
perpendicularly, and moving it, egg
and all, slowly around the jelly-glass,
" the days and nights would be of
equal length, but as it is in a slant-
ing position," sloping it accordingly,
" they are unequal except in spring
and autumn. As the Earth moves
in her path round the Sun, her axis
being slanted, she sometimes turns
the North Pole to the Sun, and
sometimes the South Pole; that is,
sometimes one end of the pencil,
and sometimes the other. When the
North Pole is inclined towards
the Sun, the Earth is in such a position that the Sun is above the horizon

in the Northern Hemisphere much
longer than he is below it, and
our days are longer than our nights.
Look, Nelly, this little bit of shell
which is still sticking to the egg,
between the top and the middle, we
will call Boston ; and you see that in
turning the egg round, with its North
Pole towards the jelly-glass, Boston
will be in the light much longer than
it is in the dark. But when the North
Pole is turned *away* from the Sun,
then he is below the horizon longer
than he is above it, which will give
our Boston long nights and short
days."

"I understand," said Harry. Nelly took a second turnover and said
nothing.

" What makes the summer days

warmer than the winter days?" asked Harry, regaining his zest for knowledge after refreshing himself with a mugful of cold coffee.

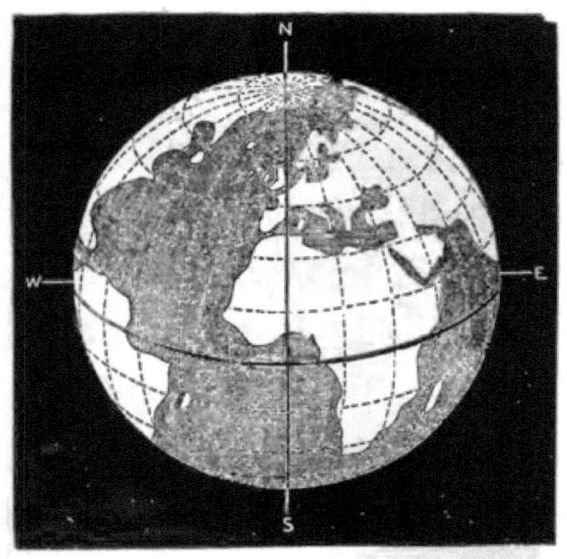

The Earth as seen from the Sun at the Summer Solstice, June 21 (noon at London).

"When the North Pole is slanted towards the Sun," explained the ever-ready Professor, "we who live in the Northern Hemisphere have our sum-

mer, for the Sun is very nearly overhead, and we have more heat from him
when he is directly above us, and his
rays come straight to us, than when
he is nearer the horizon, and the rays
come slantingly.

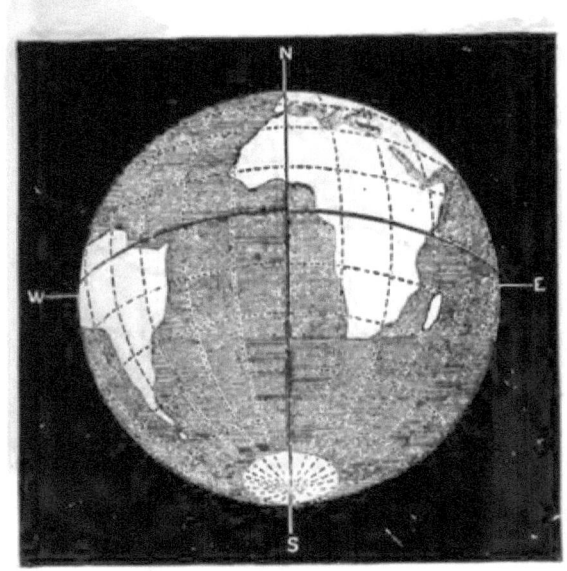

The Earth, as seen from the Sun at the Winter Solstice, Dec. 21
(noon at London).

When the *South* Pole slopes
towards the Sun, the people in the
Southern Hemisphere have *their*

summer, and we, being partly turned away from the Sun, have less heat, and we call it winter."

Here the Professor ate his egg,

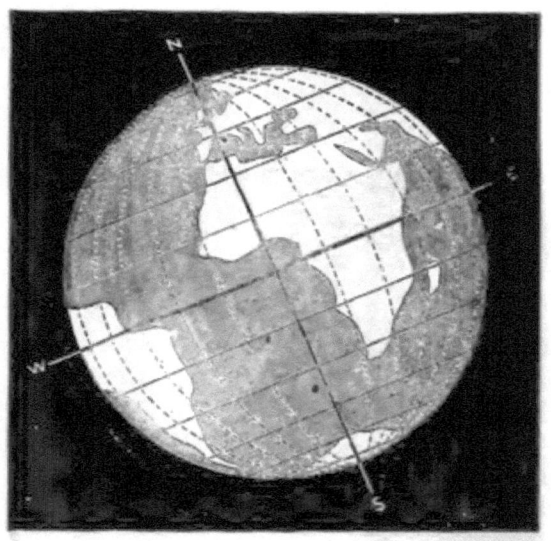

The Earth, as seen from the Sun at the Vernal Equinox, March 21 (noon at London.)

after removing Boston and the pencil, and adding a pinch of salt.

"And besides, Harry," said Miss Miranda, "the Sun hasn't time to give us much heat in the winter, he is above the horizon such a little while."

" I ought also to tell you," resumed the Professor, " that in spring and autumn, about the 21st of March, and the 21st of September, the axis

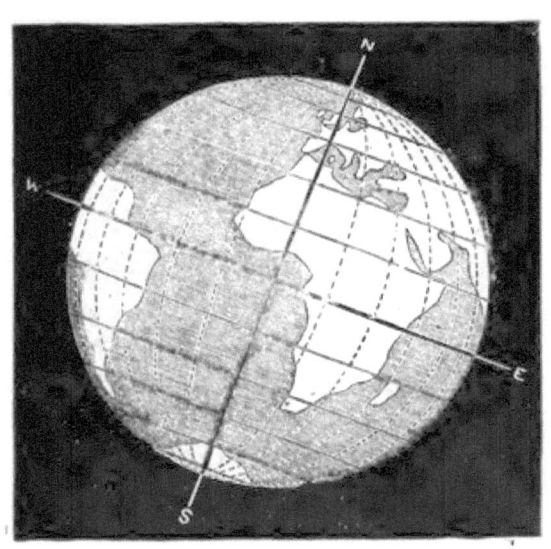

The Earth, as seen from the Sun at the Autumnal Equinox, Sept. 21 (noon at London.)

of the Earth is sloped sidewise to the Sun, so the days and nights are equal, and the weather is neither hot nor cold.   At the Equator, the Sun is nearly overhead, and it is always hot, and the days and nights are equal in length. But at the Poles, the day is six months long, that is, the Sun is in sight six months at a time, and then disappears for about six months, making both night and winter wonderful to think of."

"Only one day and one night in a whole year," said Miss Roseberry.

"What an unfortunate night that would be to have a toothache, Harry, or to wait for Christmas presents, Nelly," laughed the Professor; "but," he continued, "these long nights of the Polar regions are not as dark as our nights although they have only a faint twilight instead of the Sun — yet the Moon and Stars shine twice as brightly there, and the ice and snow reflect the light so that people can see to go about, and even to read."

" And then they have the beautiful Northern Lights," added Miss Roseberry.

" Yes," responded Dr. Willoughby, " the Aurora Borealis is far more brilliant there than we ever see it, illuminating the whole heavens with streams of red and white light, indeed of all the colors of the rainbow, and nearly as bright as our full moon."

" O, how lovely it must be!" said Nelly ; " I should like to go there."

" In midsummer," continued the Professor, " although the Sun remains visible for several months, it is not as bright in the evening as in the middle of the day, but shines with a soft radiance like our moon-light, and one can look at it without pain or injury to the eyes."

" So you can here, if you have a piece of colored glass," said Harry.

" I have sometimes thought," said Miss Roseberry, "that I would be willing to endure the hardships of an arctic voyage for the sake of seeing the Aurora in its perfection."

" Heaven forbid," said the Professor, " but it must be a magnificent sight, with its streams of varying color in incessant quivering motion. No wonder ignorant people looked upon it as a sign of coming trouble, or fancied that they saw supernatural armies contending in chariots of fire."

" You know Whittier calls it 'the

midnight sword-dance of the Northern sky,'" said Miss Roseberry.

.   .   .   .

After dinner Nelly soon followed
Abner's example, and fell fast asleep
in the shade on the pile of shawls.
Miss Roseberry sat near with the
last Atlantic Monthly in her hand,
but her eyes often wandered from
Mr. Aldrich's serial to the lovely
panorama of field, lake and forest,
spread at her feet. The Professor
ingeniously arranged an open umbrella over her by lashing it to the
branch of a tree, after which he and
Harry rambled away in search of
geological specimens, and all became
so still that the birds and squirrels
peeping out were convinced that the
late intruders were quite gone, and

they presently ventured fully forth
and began to pick up the fragments
of the feast, turning now and then
a bright, inquisitive eye upon the
umbrella, which they doubtless re-
garded as an unusually large mush-
room of surprisingly sudden growth.

Thus the afternoon passed quietly
away, until the Sun sank low, and a
cooler air began to stir the spruce
plumes.

Abner was now awake and in-
dulging in a pipe of tobacco; Nelly,
also aroused, was first hunting about
for checkerberries, then feeding Sorrel and Light-foot with tufts of grass,
chattering like a mocking-bird all the
while.

The Professor and Harry had returned with their pockets full of stony

treasures, and were eagerly display-
ing for Miss Roseberry's admiration,
clusters of clear quartz crystals, flakes
of mica two inches long, darkly glowing lumps of garnets, and fragments
of rose-colored quartz as delicately
tinted as the sunset clouds.

" I had no idea there was anything
but granite in these New Hampshire
hills," she frankly exclaimed; " I am
ashamed of my ignorance!"

Somehow the Professor was not at
all shocked; he found it decidedly
pleasant to have her honest, blue eyes
looking to him for information; he en-
joyed watching her plump, pretty
hands turning the rough stones over
and over as he told her about them.

But now the children were hungry
and thirsty again, so their elders took

the remaining cakes and sandwiches from the basket, packed the crystals, &c., carefully in their stead, and decided to postpone science till a more convenient season.

After supper, Abner harnessed the horse, packed baskets and shawls into the wagon, but failed to persuade any of his passengers to ride down the first series of rocky steeps. Miss Miranda was really afraid, Nelly thought proper to be timid too; the Professor was too gallant to desert his ladies, and Harry of course followed his example.

So Abner grinned and started alone, promising to wait for them at the watering-trough, Major after some hesitation followed him, and the colt resumed his devious devotion

to his mother. The Professor having
foreseen that Miss Roseberry would
prefer walking, had secretly looked
forward to a pleasant chat with her,
supposing the children would choose
to ride, or would ramble in advance.

He was sadly disappointed however, for Nelly was just tired enough
to cling closely to her cousin's hand,
and Harry was provokingly determined to find out all about the Moon,
which now nearly full, was rising in
rosy beauty above the distant mountains. He concealed his annoyance
as well as he could, but was not quite
amiable enough to gratify the boy's
ill-timed thirst for information.

"We've had science enough for
one day, Harry, I think," he said, "I
will tell you all I can Monday night,

when she will be quite full. Now, Miss Roseberry, you have stumbled twice, — indeed you had better take my arm, — this uncertain light makes walking dangerous on a stony road."

Miss Miranda complied rather shyly. Somehow *she* was quite willing to have the children stay. A new gentleness in the Doctor's manner suddenly made him seem less like the elderly, absent-minded scholar she had heretofore considered him. She was glad when they presently overtook Abner and the wagon; gladder still when half an hour later saw them safely alighting at Mrs. Parsnips' gate.

Why should Abner have grinned?

Chapter VI.

NEWS FROM HOME.

THE next morning's mail brought a letter from Mrs. Marlow which altered the plans of the whole party.

"You will be sorry to hear, dear Miranda," she wrote, "that your Uncle has been less and less well ever since you and the children went away, and yesterday he actually fainted in his office. You can imagine how frightened I was when he came home in a carriage, and how Dr. Bonney scowled and scolded and stamped about the room. The result is that we are to go out of town next week, and Henry is not to go near the office again till September at least. I am not sure where we shall go. For my own part I should prefer to join you and the children at Hickory Corners. Your descriptions quite fascinate me, and I know your Uncle would like that old Professor you all quote so much." Miss Rose-berry winced a little here. " However, Henry is more fond of the sea-shore than the mountains, and as the Doctor thinks bathing will be good for him, we have written to a place called Lotus Bay, where Mrs. Bon-ney went once, and liked very much. We have not had a reply yet, but if we go there, I think you and the children had better join us as soon as we are settled, say the last of this month. It seems a pity to move them when they are doing so well, but I know they will help amuse their father, and of course I do want to see them myself. You must stay as long as we do, and we will have some cosy times together."

Miss Roseberry was strangely depressed by this letter, and the worst of it was that she could not feel sure it was wholly because of her Uncle's ill-health. She had always supposed herself very fond of the sea-shore, but now she experienced no special joy in the prospect of going there. The "cosy times" at Lotus Bay did not seem to her as alluring as the study of astronomy and geology at the Widow Parsnips'.

No other letter came for several days however, and on Monday evening the full Moon and the Professor kept their appointments, and met Miss Miranda and the children on the piazza after tea.

" Now, Nelly, sit down and keep still," said Harry; " Doctor Willoughby's going to tell us all about the Moon."

"Come and see the Moon, Kitty," said Nelly, catching up the unwilling cat as she obeyed Harry.

" Perhaps she had rather see the Milky-way," said Miss Roseberry.

At all events Kitty would not be coaxed to remain, and presently capered away in pursuit of a large cricket.

" What is the Milky-way ? " asked Nelly, resigning herself.

" I know," said Harry; " it's that

sort of whitish cloud that stretches over the sky sometimes. You can't see it now. I suppose the Moon's too bright to let it show. It's all made up of little bits of stars."

"Millions and millions of them," said the Professor. "Galileo discovered that with his wonderful telescope."

"O, how big the Moon is!" exclaimed Nelly, suddenly changing the subject. "It looks as big as the Sun!"

"So it does, Nelly," said the Professor, "and yet it is smaller than any of the stars. It is about a third as large as Mercury, and its diameter a little more than one fourth of the diameter of the Earth. Why do you suppose it looks so large?"

"Something the matter with our eyes?" ventured Nelly.

"O, no!" said Harry, "it's because it's so near, isn't it?"

"You are right, Harry," said the Doctor; "it is nearer us than any of the heavenly bodies. Instead of being millions of miles away, it is less than a quarter of a million of miles from us."

"Going to the Moon would be equal to traveling round the Earth nine or ten times then," said Miss Roseberry.

"I wish I knew how far a million of miles would seem," interrupted Harry, before Dr. Willoughby could reply to his cousin.

"It would take nearly four years to travel a million of miles," responded the Professor, "even if you traveled day and night, and at the rate of thirty miles an hour."

" Only think what a long journey, Harry," said Miss Roseberry; "you would be almost a man before you arrived."

" I should like that," said Harry.

" Is there really a man in the Moon ? " asked Nelly. " Abner said ———."

"O, no, Nelly," cried Harry, scornfully; "Abner was only in fun ; but Dr. Willoughby do you think there are any people there ?"

" It seems unlikely," was the reply. " If there are inhabitants, they must be entirely different from us. There is no water on the Moon, and no air ———."

"O, dear," gasped both the children.

" And according to all accounts no vegetation ; and then, in the Moon's journey round the Sun, she has alternately a fortnight of intense heat, greater than at our Equator, and a fortnight of extreme cold, more severe than that of our Polar regions, so it would not be a very comfortable place to live in."

The children sat in amazed silence.

" How very inconvenient too," said Miss Roseberry ; " just fancy, Nelly, having all your furs and blankets and buffalo-robes and furnace-fires in use one week, and the next rushing into muslin dresses, putting up mosquito curtains, sending out for ice-cream and fans, and hating the very sight of woolen carpets !"

" That is a domestic view of the

case that had not occurred to me," laughed the Professor.

" How will the Moon look when we see it through the telescope ? " pursued the ever practical Harry.

" The surface seems rough and desolate," replied the Professor, " and covered with spots, some dusky and some bright. The ancient astronomers supposed the dusky spots to be seas, and gave them names which are still retained on the maps. One is called the Sea of Nectar, another the Sea of Tranquillity, &c., but these spots are now thought to be plains, and the bright ones mountains."

" Why do they think they are mountains ? " asked Harry.

" From the shadows they cast when the Sun shines upon them," replied his friend, "and some of them are more than twenty thousand feet high."

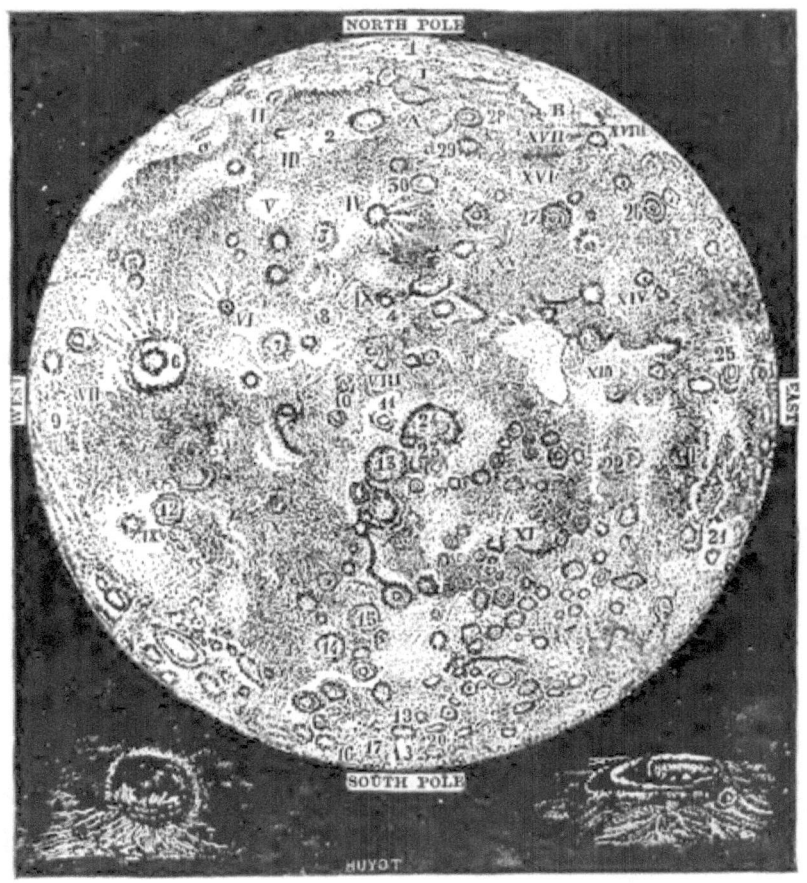

The Moon.

" They are of volcanic origin, are they not," inquired Miss Roseberry,

anxious to atone for her recent friv-
olous remarks.

"Yes," he returned; "the theory
is, that both the Earth and the Moon
were once glowing stars. After a
time the surface of the Earth began
to cool and form a crust, and this
crust gradually grew thicker and
thicker, till now it is thick enough
and cool enough for us to live upon.
But the centre of the Earth is supposed to be still glowing, and the
books say that at the depth of twenty
miles the ground is doubtless red-
hot. Earthquakes are caused by the
gas and steam shut up under the
crust, and volcanoes are the safety-
valves for their escape."

"How dreadful that seems!"
sighed Nelly, looking anxiously

A Lunar Landscape.

around as if expecting one in Abner's cornfield at once.

"I've seen the steam come bubbling up through the crust on top of the hasty-pudding when Mrs. Parsnips is making it for breakfast," said Harry. "Sometimes she lets me watch it and stir it for fear it will burn, and it makes a funny, puffing noise, and looks just like little volcanoes. Once I burnt my hand by letting it go too near when one of them burst and spit out the steam."

"That is a capital illustration, Harry," said the Professor, smiling, and nodding at Miss Roseberry over Harry's head.

"These Moon volcanoes are supposed to have done sputtering and steaming, but there are streaks or rays of light extending from them that look like streams of cooled lava. One of these mountains or craters called Copernicus, is more than fifty miles in diameter, and the walls of it rise eleven thousand feet above the surrounding plains."

" How tantalizing it is never to see the other side of the Moon," said Miss Roseberry.

" But the people on the other side, if there are any, can see our Earth by making a little journey across their rugged mountains to this side," said the Professor.

" Doesn't the Moon turn round like the Earth so we can see both sides of it ? " asked Harry.

" She turns around," replied the Professor, " but as it takes her just

The Earth, as seen from the Moon.

as long to turn on her axis as it does to go round the Earth, we always see the same side. Try it for yourself, Harry. Take hold of that little elm-tree with your hands, and go around it, keeping your face towards it all the time. You see you turn completely round every time you go round the tree. When you began you were facing me, when you had gone half round your back was turned towards me, and now you have gone entirely round, you are facing me again."

"Yes, I think I understand it," said Harry, "but how can they be sure it is always the same side?"

"By the spots on the surface," answered Dr. Willoughby, "we always see the same mountains and valleys whenever we look at the Moon, that is, when she turns her bright side towards us."

"O, see what a black cloud is coming!" cried Nelly, "it's covered up ever so many stars already, and I b'lieve it 'll hide our lovely Moon in a minute."

Nelly was right. With a suddenness that surprised them all, the beautiful subject of their conversation was presently obscured; a cold wind came down from the mountains behind the house, and presently doors began to slam, and a low muttering of thunder was heard.

"How chilly it has grown," said Miss Roseberry, as they all hurried into the parlor; "we are like the

Moon-people when their frosty fort-night has begun."

In another moment the rain poured down, and they had to close the windows, but the Professor brought in his cheerful student-lamp, and they finished the evening merrily, playing "Twenty Questions."

CHAPTER VII.

MORE ABOUT THE MOON.

THE next evening being clear, Harry asked the Professor to go on with the "Moon-talk," as he called it, and Miss Roseberry and Nelly having been summoned, they seated themselves on the piazza as before, and watched the beautiful orb as she slowly rose above the pine-fringed hills.

"It is not quite as round as it was last night," said Harry, breaking the silence at last.

"No," said Dr. Willoughby, "it cannot be perfect long; it has begun to wane already." He spoke soberly, and glanced at Miss Roseberry.

"Why isn't it full Moon all the time?" demanded Nelly, to her cousin's relief, for she was uncomfortably aware that she too was thinking how a pleasant vacation might begin to wane just as it reached perfection.

" It's a great deal prettier to have it round," added the child.

" Don't you like to see the little new Moon sometimes, Nelly?" asked Miss Roseberry, " and the old Moon in the new Moon's arms that I showed you once ?"

" Yes, pretty well," said Nelly, "but I like the full Moon better. It makes it so light."

" Perhaps," said Miss Roseberry, " it will please you to know that when the dark side of the Moon is turned toward us the bright side of our Earth is turned toward the Moon; so if there are any little girls there they have then a big, bright Earth to light them."

"And *full Earth* is about thirteen times larger than full Moon," added the Professor.

" Let me see," said Harry, trying to explain the matter clearly to himself, " if the Sun was over there and the Moon was between the Sun and us, the side of the Moon that was turned toward the Sun would be bright of course, because the Sun would be shining straight on it, but the side toward us would be all dark and cold because it was out of sight of the Sun."

" Yes," said Dr. Willoughby, " the Moon has no light of her own. She is only bright when the Sun shines upon her. When she is between us and the Sun, her dark side is toward us. So then we cannot see her, but

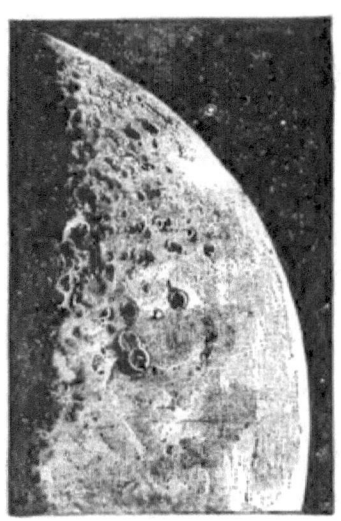

The lunar crescent six days after a new Moon.

as she moves along in her path around our Earth, she soon comes into such a position that she shows us a little strip of her bright side. This is the small crescent we see in the south-western sky soon after sunset, and which we call the new Moon. Every night this crescent grows broader as the Moon travels along her path, — in fact *crescent* is from a Latin word which means to increase———."

" Yes, yes," cried Harry, " I know in my music lesson it says 'crescendo,' when I ought to play louder."

" Good!" cried Dr. Willoughby, much pleased; " it is a comfort to teach such a boy as you, Harry.

Harry blushed hotly at this praise, and snuggled a little closer to his friend in grateful acknowledgment of his approval, but he said nothing, and the Professor presently continued: "At last when the Moon is on the other side of us so that she is op-

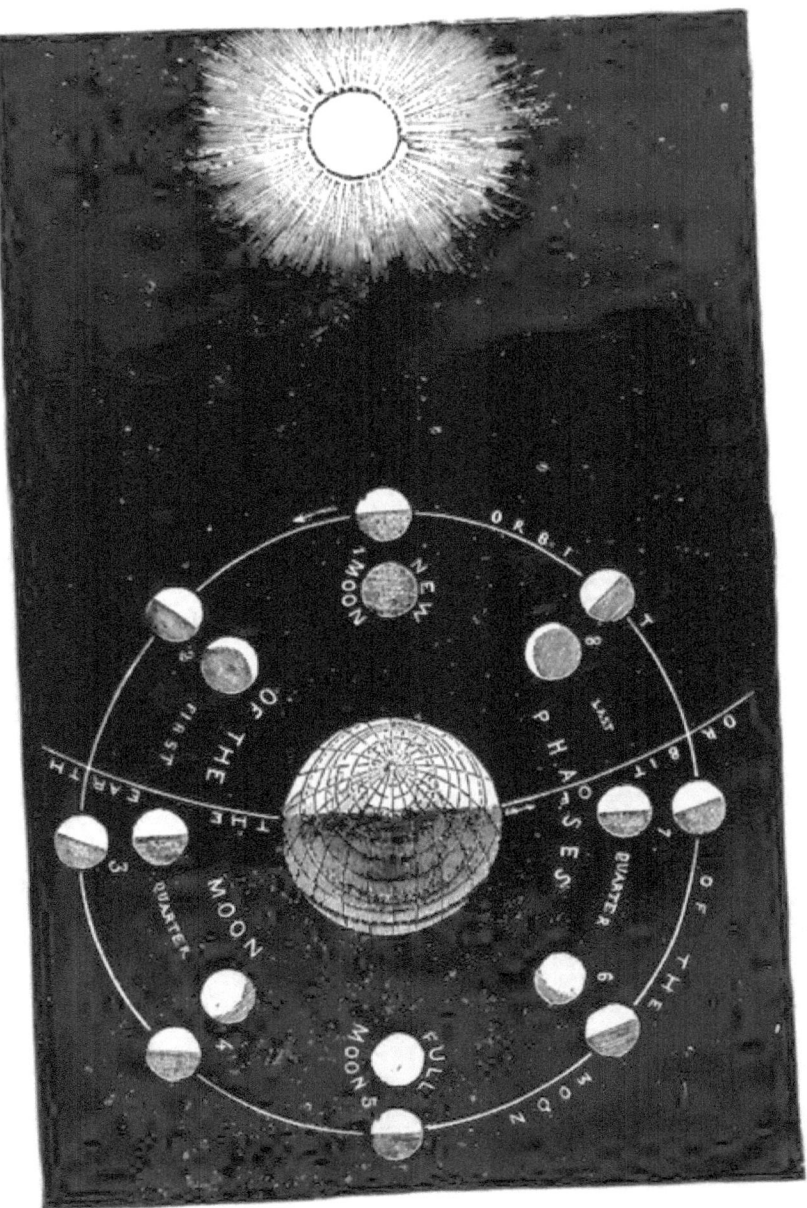

The Moon's phases.

posite the Sun, her whole bright side
is turned toward us as it was last
night, and we call it *full Moon.*
Then she gradually grows smaller

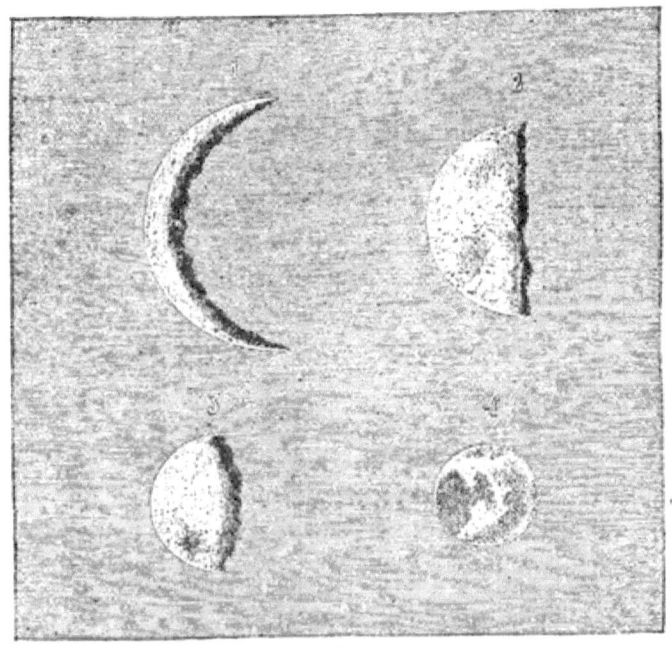

The phases of Venus.

as she moves along, until she dwin-
dles to a small rim again. She is
about twenty-nine and a half days in
passing through these changes, or

phases, as they are called; and our
Earth goes through the same changes,
or would appear to do so, to an ob-
server on the Moon.   Venus and
Mercury have similar phases."

The phases of Mercury.

" What we call the ' old Moon in
the new Moon's arms,' is caused by

the ' Earth-shine,' isn't it ? " asked
Miss Roseberry.

" Yes," replied the Professor, " the
bright crescent is where the sunlight
strikes the Moon, and the Earth
throws a faint light reflected from
the Sun upon the rest of the Moon,
just enough to make it vaguely visible."

" If the Earth is in between the Sun
and the Moon now, why isn't there
an eclipse to-night ?" asked Harry.

" Because the Moon's path is not
exactly level with the path of the
Earth," responded the Professor.

" If it were we should have an
eclipse every time the Moon came
between the Earth and the Sun, and
every time the Earth came between
the Sun and the Moon ; but the

Moon's path is sloped or tilted slightly, so that she sometimes passes a little too high, and sometimes a little too low to bring her just on a line with the Sun and the Earth, and therefore we do not have an eclipse then."

"I wish I could see an eclipse of the Sun," said Harry; "is it very dark when the Sun is behind the Moon?"

"It is not dark like night," replied the Professor, "but there is a strange unnatural gloom over everything; animals seem frightened and confused as the darkness comes on, and birds put their heads under their wings and go to sleep. In old times people were very much alarmed when an eclipse took place. They thought something terrible was about to happen. Some nations believed that the Sun and Moon veiled their faces because they were offended, and would try in various ways to conciliate them. In the East Indies the natives imagined that a great dragon was flying through the air, and clutching at the Sun and Moon with his black claws."

" I've read a first-rate story about an eclipse," said Harry. " It says that Christopher Columbus and his men were nearly starved one time, and the Indians wouldn't bring them any food, and Columbus happened to remember there was going to be an eclipse of the Moon that very night, so he thought he'd scare the Indians with it, and he called the chiefs and told them if they didn't bring him food, the light of the Moon should be taken away from them. By and by the eclipse began, and the Indians were dreadfully frightened, and they ran to Columbus and begged him to let the Moon shine again. So he went into his tent, or somewhere out of sight, and pretended to be doing something about it till the eclipse was over, and the Moon shone out as bright as ever. Then the Indians were so glad that they promised to do just whatever he told them to."

"So they brought him some food?" said Nelly, eagerly.

"Of course," said Harry.

"I knew a little boy once," said Miss Roseberry, "who saw the Moon

when it was full, and then again when
it was a new Moon, and he was quite
distressed to see it so small, for he

Kitty Gray.

thought some one had broken it.
But when he saw it full again, he
was delighted, and cried out: ' O,

papa has mended the Moon! papa has mended the Moon!"

"I suppose his father used to mend his playthings for him," said Nelly, "but he must have been very small and foolish."

"It must seem wonderful to uneducated people that eclipses can be so accurately foretold," remarked Miss Roseberry, after a pause.

"Yes," said Dr. Willoughby, "and that gives me a chance to tell a story. Once there was a Danish boy, Nelly, named Tycho Brahe."

"I don't like his name very well," said Nelly, severely.

"I have heard prettier ones myself," said the Professor. "When Tycho was about fourteen, a total eclipse of the Sun was predicted for

EFFICIES TICHONIS BRAHE OTTONI DA
ÆTATIS SVÆ ANNOSQ.COMPLETO

QVO POST DIVTINVM IN PATRIA
EXILIVM LIBERTATI DESIDERATÆ
DIVINO PROVISV
RESTITVTVS EST

Portrait of Tycho Brahe (from original painting in the possession of
Dr. Crompton, of Manchester).

a certain day and hour, and when he saw the Sun obscured at exactly the moment named in the astrological almanac, he was so filled with astonishment and admiration that he determined to devote himself to the study of astronomy."

" And did he ?" asked Nelly.

" Yes," replied the Professor; "the king of Denmark built him a magnificent Observatory on the island of Huen, between Denmark and Sweden. He called this *Uraniberg*, or the city of the Heavens, and here, during twenty-one years, he carefully watched the stars, and made many valuable observations which have been of great use to those who came after him. His friend and pupil, John Kepler, was also one of the greatest of astronomers, and was led to make some of his most important discoveries by Tycho Brahe's observations."

"That's what I'm going to be when I grow up," said Harry.

"I don't believe President Hayes will build you an Observatory anywhere," said Nelly, who was getting tired and a little cross.

"Of course not you goosey!" retorted Harry; "Hayes won't be President when I'm grown up."

"Well, I hope nobody will," said Nelly, who did not like to be called a "goosey." "Just think how tired that Tycho must have been! Studying twenty-one years! I know you'd be as cross as anything!"

"I'm afraid that means that I've tired you, Nelly," said the Professor,

Tycho Brahe's Observatory on the Island of Huen.

Monument erected to Kepler at Weildiestadt, his native town.

kindly; "we have had wise talk enough for one evening. Run and get your bean-bag, and let us see if you can catch it forty times without missing before 'Cousin Miranda' begins to look at her watch and talk about bed-time."

The evening ended cheerfully, but the next morning Miss Roseberry saw Dr. Willoughby returning from the Post-office with such a slow step and melancholy expression that she felt sure he had received some bad news.

When she met him at the door, however, he only gave her a letter from Mrs. Marlow, saying: "This is our whole mail to-day." It contained, as she and he feared, a summons to Lotus Bay. They must start on Friday at the latest, Mr. and Mrs. Marlow being already there, and pleased with the place.

Friday came all too soon. Mrs. Parsnips loudly lamented the departure of the "best boarders she had ever had," while the Professor's silence expressed even more.

Even Abner seemed sorry to say good-bye, and as he shouldered the trunks, awkwardly expressed a hope that he should " have the heftin' on 'em again next summer."

Mrs. Parsnips consoled herself by packing a basket of luncheon large enough for three days rations, and by sending a box of honey to Mr. Marlow.

The Professor said very little, but walked to the station with them, and as he shook hands with all in parting, said :

" I'm sorry I haven't been able to keep my promise about the telescope, Harry: " what do you say to going to Cambridge for a day with me if I can run down to the Cape for you ?"

" O, goody !" cried Harry, forgetting his dignity for a moment, and fairly blushing with pleasure at the thought. Oddly enough, the Professor looked at Miss Roseberry instead of at the boy, and she was blushing too.

Then the train rushed up, and away they went, leaving the Professor smiling and waving his hat, while Abner grinned in the background as he took up the handles of his wheelbarrow.

Chapter VIII.

LETTERS.

Letter from Prof. Willoughby to Harry.

Dear Harry:

Mrs. Parsnips desires me to acknowledge the receipt of a postal card which has just reached her, with the welcome news that you all arrived safely in Boston, and were about starting for Cape Cod.

I remembered your hand-writing, but Mrs. Parsnips, with that greater keenness which belongs to ladies, recognized it as Miss Miranda's suggestion, and bids me say "she is the thoughtfullest lady I ever did see, and it's just like her."

We have missed you all very much ; even Major looks dejected, and that reminds me of something strange that happened the day you left.

On returning from the station, I took my book and camp chair to the barn in search of a breeze. Kitty Gray was curled up on the hay, and presently Major came in, panting from his walk to the station, and from chasing a woodchuck on his way home. I shut my eyes and kept quiet, knowing he would tease me to go to walk if he thought me awake. He respected my apparent nap, and lay down at the foot of the ladder which led to Kitty's nest. Presently I heard her say :

" How foolish you were to go to the village this hot day!"

" I wanted to see the boarders off," replied Major.

" What a fuss you make about them," returned Puss.

" Because I'm sorry to have them go, aren't you?" inquired the honest dog.

" Not very," said Kitty.

" Don't you like them?" said Major; " for my part I wish it was next summer, and they were here again."

" I don't," said Kitty; "do you suppose I like to be wrapped up in a shawl to play I am a sick child, and have my tail pinched to make me cry? And then I never could get a chance to catch a mouse except at night. What's the use of sitting quietly by a mouse-hole if a little girl comes and sits down by you and talks all the time and frightens the mouse away? What they said about the Milky-way too! That's the milk-room I suppose, but they needn't have said anything about it! I hardly ever do anything but lick the outside of the pans."

" O, Kitty!" said Major, "didn't I see you the other day with cream on your smellers?"

" They're not smellers, they're whiskers," retorted Kitty, and ended the discussion by walking away. This amused me so that I felt as much refreshed as if I had had a nap, and accordingly I invited Major, and we took a long tramp.

When I told Mrs. Parsnips at tea
what I had overheard, she was unkind
enough to laugh and call it a dream,
but I look for more sympathy from
you and Nelly.

If you should be dull before you
feel at home at Lotus Bay, or be
home-sick for Hickory Corners as
you said you should, let me advise
you to begin a collection of some
sort : birds' eggs or birds' nests, post-
age stamps, shells, seaweeds, — no
matter what, you will find it an excel-
lent remedy for ennui. You see I do
not hesitate to use a hard word, for I
know you will look it out in the dic-
tionary, or ask your cousin, and so
the more I use, the more you will
learn.   I have begun a collection of
minerals since you left, to astonish

Miss Roseberry with the wealth of New Hampshire, if she comes here next summer. Some rainy day when you cannot go out, and your father is reading and Nelly at her lessons, I hope you will write to your friend, the old hermit of Hickory Corners, and tell him all you are seeing and doing.

I expect to go to Boston early next month to see the occulist, and may then run down to Cape Cod to see you. Present my respects to your parents, and remember me cordially to Miss Miranda and Nelly.

Your sincere friend,
JOHN WILLOUGHBY.

Harry read his letter with a smiling face, and then gave it to Miss Roseberry, saying : " There's a message for you, and you can read it all if you choose."

" Read it aloud," said Mrs. Marlow; " I should like to judge of the man who has bewitched you all so."

Miss Miranda's cheeks reddened, but she went bravely through the letter, and they all laughed heartily at the kitten talk.

" I should say he was a very clever fellow," said Mr. Marlow, " and I only wish he may come down here to wake us all up."

" I don't wonder Harry gave you the letter, Miranda," was Mrs. Marlow's only comment ; " it's evidently written especially for you."

Fortunately Harry had left the

room. Miss Roseberry, whose cheeks were painfully red now, only laughed and said, " Nonsense."

Letter from Harry to Professor Willoughby.

LOTUS BAY, July, 1877.

Dear Dr. Willoughby:

It is a very stormy day, just as you told me, and papa is playing chess with Cousin Miranda, and Nelly is in the kitchen helping the girl make doughnuts, so that is all right, isn't it? I thank you very much for your letter, and we all laughed about Major and Kitty.

O, I must not forget to tell you we are all making collections, papa said it was such a good idea. He misses his office and the reading-room you know, and mamma has no

callers here, and I mustn't read, and
Nelly hasn't any girls to play with,
and I don't know what Cousin
Miranda misses, but she is collecting
too. You would never guess what
they all are, so I'll tell you. Father's
is Indian names of places that he
hears the people here talk about.
Some are so funny. Cuttyhunk and
Pennikese, and Cooneymasset and
Squiteague and Siasconsett, but it's
too hard work to stop and ask how
to spell them, and you can see papa's
list when you come.

Mamma is getting a lot of rules
for cake and pudding, and Nelly is
collecting scallop-shells, and I help
her, and we've got ninety-four, no
two alike, all on a beam in the barn,
and besides I am collecting coins.

I've got copper cents of fifteen different years, and twelve foreign coins. You know there are ever so many old sea-captains here, and they get them.

Cousin Miranda's collection is wild-flowers, and she presses one of every kind. She found over forty kinds the first walk we took.

You shall see everything when you come, and we all hope you will. Father says so too.

Your friend,
HARRY MARLOW.

Chapter IX

THE PROFESSOR'S VISIT.

N the course of the next week, Harry received a second letter from Prof. Willoughby.

Though it contained but a few lines, it pleased him more than the first, for it said: "I expect to arrive at the Pokonoket House next Thursday, and hope to drive over to Lotus Bay the following afternoon.

"O, papa! You will be glad to see him, won't you?" cried Harry, as soon as he had read this aloud.

"And you'll make him stay to tea won't you, mamma? O, Cousin

Miranda! won't it be fun to see him again? We'll take him to walk with us, and fishing, and bathing, and clamming, and scalloping, and every-thing — and you shall go too, Nelly," he generously added, seeing her eyes grow round and eager.

"All that in one afternoon, Har-ry?" cried Miss Roseberry, laughing, and Mrs. Marlow thought she looked quite as happy over the news as the children did.

Punctually on the appointed day the Professor arrived looking remark-ably spruce and beamingly happy. Nelly flung herself upon him, and offered a kiss as soon as he jumped from the buggy, while Harry secured his right hand, and led him eagerly toward Mr. Marlow, who advanced from the house to be introduced. Mrs. Marlow and Miss Roseberry were found in the parlor, and all were soon chatting like old friends.

"How nice you look in a white vest," exclaimed Nelly, in a pause of the conversation; "you never wore one at Mrs. Parsnips'?"

"Perhaps I did not want to outshine Abner's spotted one," answered the Professor, and hastened to change the subject before the child could comment upon his new Panama hat, or the spray of coral-colored Bavardia in his button-hole.

"Are you not going to show me your scallop-shells, Nelly?" he said.

"O, yes," she cried, "and then will you go on the beach with us?"

He willingly consented, and asked

if all the party would not go too.
Mr. Marlow declined, as it was his
hour for a nap, and Mrs. Marlow
wished to remain with him, but
Miss Roseberry was at leisure, and
presently she and Harry, Nelly and
the Professor started together along
the winding path, through grassy
fields, toward the sea. On reaching
a picturesque point, Miss Roseberry
and the Professor sat down to rest
upon the rocks, while Harry and
Nelly wandered away to search for
scallop-shells. They had rambled
some distance, when Harry, who
was considerably in advance, heard
Nelly crying, and ran back to see
what was the matter. She was
dancing up and down in much
distress, and pointing at her basket,

which was floating far away upon the waves.

"O dear, O dear!" she sobbed; "my nice little red and white basket! I only left it a few minutes, and now it's sailing and sailing, and I know it will never come back. What shall I do?"

"You can't do anything," said Harry, "you'll have to let it sail away. Perhaps the tide will bring it back, or perhaps it will take it somewhere else, and then some other little girl will have it for her dear red and white basket."

"O, Harry! how unkind you are," cried his sister. "I don't like this beach at all! I like the pond at Hickory Corners, where the water stays in the same place, and doesn't come up and carry things off so !"

" It's the Moon's fault," responded Harry.

" There isn't any Moon ; it's day-time," exclaimed Nelly, looking up at the sky to assure herself that she was right ; " how can you tell such a story ?"

" I'm not telling a story," said Harry, indignantly; "Captain Kidds told me so : he says it's the Moon that makes the tide come in and go out. It's high tide and low tide twice every twenty-four hours, and when it's rising they call it flood tide, and when it's falling it's ebb tide, and he was going to tell me more, but some-body called him away, so I must ask Dr. Willoughby to tell the rest.

Come, Nelly, your basket's gone, and I *am* sorry, but don't be a baby about it, come."

Nelly gave one mournful look at the far away black speck, which was now all that remained of her treasure, wiped her eyes, and followed her brother.

" Cousin Miranda," she cried, as they came near the others, " the waves came and sailed away my basket, and Harry says it's the Moon."

" Doctor Willoughby," interrupted Harry, " doesn't the Moon make the tides ? '

" The Sun and the Moon together," replied the Professor, " pull or attract the water on the Earth's surface, and make it rise up in a big wave. Can you think why the water is not drawn away from the Earth entirely ? "

" If it were, your basket would go up to the Moon too, Nelly," said Miss Roseberry, hoping to cheer the child, who still looked sober over her loss.

" Is it Attraction that you told us about once that keeps it ? " asked Harry.

" Yes," replied the Professor, " the Earth attracts the water, and keeps it from being drawn away entirely by the Sun or Moon. The Moon being nearer to the Earth, pulls harder, and raises bigger waves than the Sun although she is so much smaller. When the Sun and Moon are on the same side of the Earth, as at new

Moon, or on opposite sides, as at full Moon, they pull together, and then we have very high tides, which are called spring tides."

"I think it was a spring tide that carried away my basket," said Nelly. I'm sure it was a nice dry place where I put it down, and I only forgot it a very little while."

This was whispered in Miss Roseberry's ear, — the Professor did not hear it, so he went on:

"When the Sun is on one side of the Earth, and the Moon about half-way round toward the opposite side, they pull against each other, and the water does not rise as high in either direction as it does when they are in a line. These are called neap tides. It is observed that when it is high

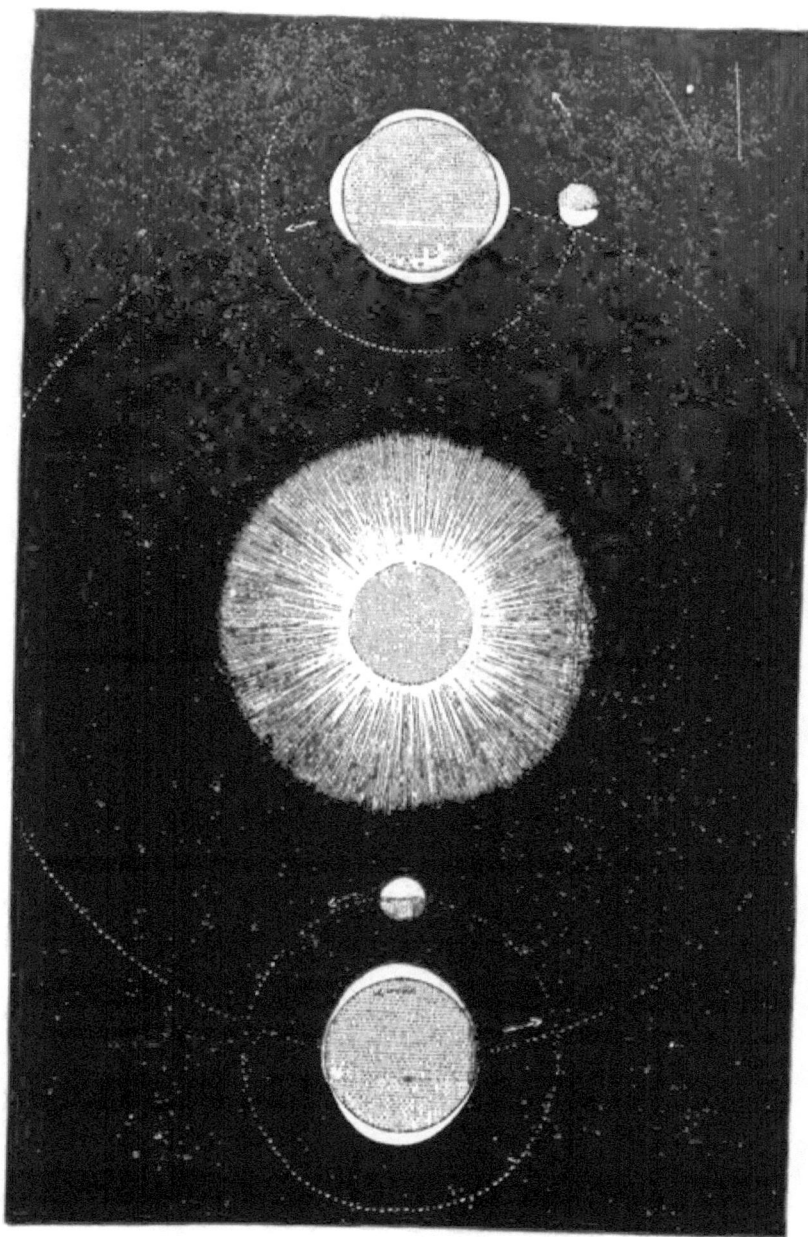

The phenomena of tides.

tide on one side of the Earth, it is always high tide at the same time on the opposite side."

" Why is it ?" asked Harry.

" It is so difficult to explain," said the Professor, "that I must ask you to remember the fact, and wait for the reasons till you are older. Perhaps by that time some better way of explaining it may be discovered."

"Captain Kidds, who lives next door to us here, says the tide rises a great deal higher in some places than in others," remarked Harry after a pause, during which they all walked along the beach.

" O, yes," responded Prof. Willoughby, " in the Bay of Fundy, where the sea runs up into a long bay, the tide rises sixty or seventy feet, and often carries away sheep and cattle it comes so fast."

" O, I hope we never shall go there to board," said Nelly, looking nervously toward the waves.

" In Boston it only rises about eleven feet, and in some places only eighteen inches," resumed the Professor.

" I think there is little or no tide on the Mediterranean Sea," said Miss Roseberry.

" Then let us go there," said Nelly.

" Captain Kidds says that high tide comes about fifty minutes later every day," said Harry ; " is that because the Moon rises about so much later every evening ? "

" Yes," said the Professor, " and

sometimes a strong wind blowing against the tide will delay it, or a rough irregular coast will affect it in the same way."

" O, there's a lovely white scallop-shell," cried Nelly, and just then Miss Roseberry found a pretty gray one, which excited Harry's emulation, and presently they all four were busily hunting for the same thing, and talked no more science that day.

Mrs. Marlow did invite the Professor to stay to tea, and during the evening he made so pleasant an impression upon both the parents that they urged him to come to Lotus Bay as often as he could.

After he was gone, Miss Roseberry told Harry that the oculist had reported very favorably upon Dr. Willoughby's eyes, and promised him entire cure if he would be prudent a few months more.

" O, good ! " cried Harry.

" That must have been the reason he looked so happy and smiling to-day. I supposed it was just because he was glad to see us again."

" Perhaps it was both," said Miss Roseberry.

This little conversation was on the door-step, where Miranda and Harry were fond of sitting in the evening to watch the stars and listen to the frogs in the Flax-pond over the hill.

" Miranda," interrupted Mrs. Marlow, from the sitting-room behind them, " one of us ought to go to Boston to-morrow. Henry's tonic is almost out; I want the second volume of 'Daniel Deronda,' and Harry ought to be fitted to a new pair of shoes, and have his hair cut too. Should you mind going? You know Henry hates to have me leave him so."

"O, no," said Miranda, cheerfully; "I should rather like it. I have several errands of my own."

"And I can go to-morrow too," said Harry, gravely, "for Dr. Willoughby can't come over till day after; he said he had some business to attend to to-morrow."

So it was arranged, and the two took the nine o'clock train next morning, the weather proving clear and fine. When the cars stopped at Pokonoket Station, they were very much surprised to see the Professor getting in. I think they were pleased too. The Professor certainly was, for when he saw them he exclaimed : " What a lucky man I am! Here I was dreading the tedious car-ride, and a day in town, and now I am to have such good company."

He took the seat in front of them, and the three had so much pleasant talk, that the two hours journey seemed nothing at all. On reaching town they separated, but agreed to meet again at a certain picture gallery near Park Street Church, when their respective errands were accomplished, and go thence together to take the four o'clock train for Cape Cod.

About two, accordingly, Miss Rose-

berry and Harry entered the gallery
and found the Professor waiting for
them.   They spent some time studying the paintings and engravings, but
Harry grew tired, and went to the
window to watch the crowd of pass-
ers-by on Tremont Street and the
opposite Mall. The Common looked
very lovely, with its vividly green
grass, shady avenues, noble elms, and
the clear blue and white background
of summer sky.   A man, with a
streaming cluster of red and blue gas
balloons was walking slowly up and
down, but Harry was too old to care
for him, or for the Punch and Judy
show that drew a group around it
in another place. Suddenly his quick
eyes saw something more interesting,
and he sprang back from the win-

dow crying, " O, Dr. Willoughby!
There's a man over here with a big
telescope! Can't we go and look
through it, Cousin Miranda? You
know we were disappointed about
the one at Hickory Corners!"

"Certainly," said his cousin, " if
there is time," and she looked at the
Professor. He was willing too, and
Harry eagerly led the way down-
stairs and across the street to the
corner of the Mall, where stood a
man with a large telescope, waiting
for customers. On a placard which
hung from the instrument were the
words, "Sun spot now visible."

"We have come at a fortunate
time, Harry," said the Professor.

" I only wish Nelly were here too,"
said Miranda.

The man now adjusted the glass, and they all looked through it in turn. They saw a bright disc, with a dark spot in the centre.

" That spot looks nearly as large as a pea," said Harry.

" It is probably seven thousand

miles in diameter," said the man, " but at the distance of ninety-one millions of miles, it looks small of course."

" Is it a cloud, or what is it ? " asked Harry.

" It is an opening in the bright clouds that surround the Sun, and the dark body of the Sun shows through," replied the man. Then he screwed on another eye-piece of greater power, and they looked again and saw a faint shadow round the spot. " The dark centre is called the Umbra, and the gray, shadowy part the Penumbra," he continued. " If you will come some evening I can show you the moon, or Jupiter and his Satellites."

" O, that would be nice," said Harry, " but how do you bring this telescope ?"

" I carry it myself," was the reply.

" Isn't it very heavy," said Miss Roseberry, quite shocked.

" It weighs one hundred and eighty pounds," said the man, " but that's nothing when you are used to it."

" What is it made of ? " asked
Harry.

" The tube is mahogany," replied
the man. " It is a refracting telescope, and cost me $1.500."

" How large is the object-glass ? "
inquired Dr. Willoughby.

" Eight inches," said the owner.
" Here are some curiosities," he
added, showing them, under a mi-
croscope, a few drops of stagnant
water containing a number of Hair-
worms. They looked several inches
long, and about as large round as
Miss Roseberry's little finger.

" And here," continued the show-
man, " is a small quantity of swamp-
water containing specimens of the
shell-backed Cyclops. They have
only one eye."

" What lively little creatures," said
Miranda. " They seem to swim
with those little feelers near their
heads," said Harry, when he looked;
" and now they're eating something,
and one drove the other right away."

" That is a piece of a Hair-worm
they are eating," said the man, " they
are so voracious they will eat a whole
one in a short time."

" How large are these brisk little
creatures ? " asked Miss Roseberry.

" Not half as large as the head of
a common pin," he replied, " and
the Hair-worm is about three quar-
ters of an inch long."

" I should think the worm ought
to eat the other fellow, if he is the
biggest," said Harry, after they had
paid, and thanked the man, and were

Great Silver-on-Glass Reflector at the Paris Observatory.

175

sitting under a tree, having yet half an hour before they need go to the railway-station.

"What did he mean by a Refracting telescope?" asked Harry.

"There are two kinds of Telescopes," replied the Professor, "Refractors and Reflectors. In a Reflector the rays of light are reflected from a large mirror at the lower end of the tube. The observer looking in at the upper end of the tube, stands with his back to the Sun or Moon, or whatever he wishes to look at, and sees the image reflected in the mirror. In the Refractor the object-glass refracts or bends the rays of light, and brings them to a point or focus. You will understand this better when you study the science of Optics."

"What is an Object-glass?" asked Harry.

The Washington Great Equatorial.

"It is the glass at the large end of the tube next to the object to be

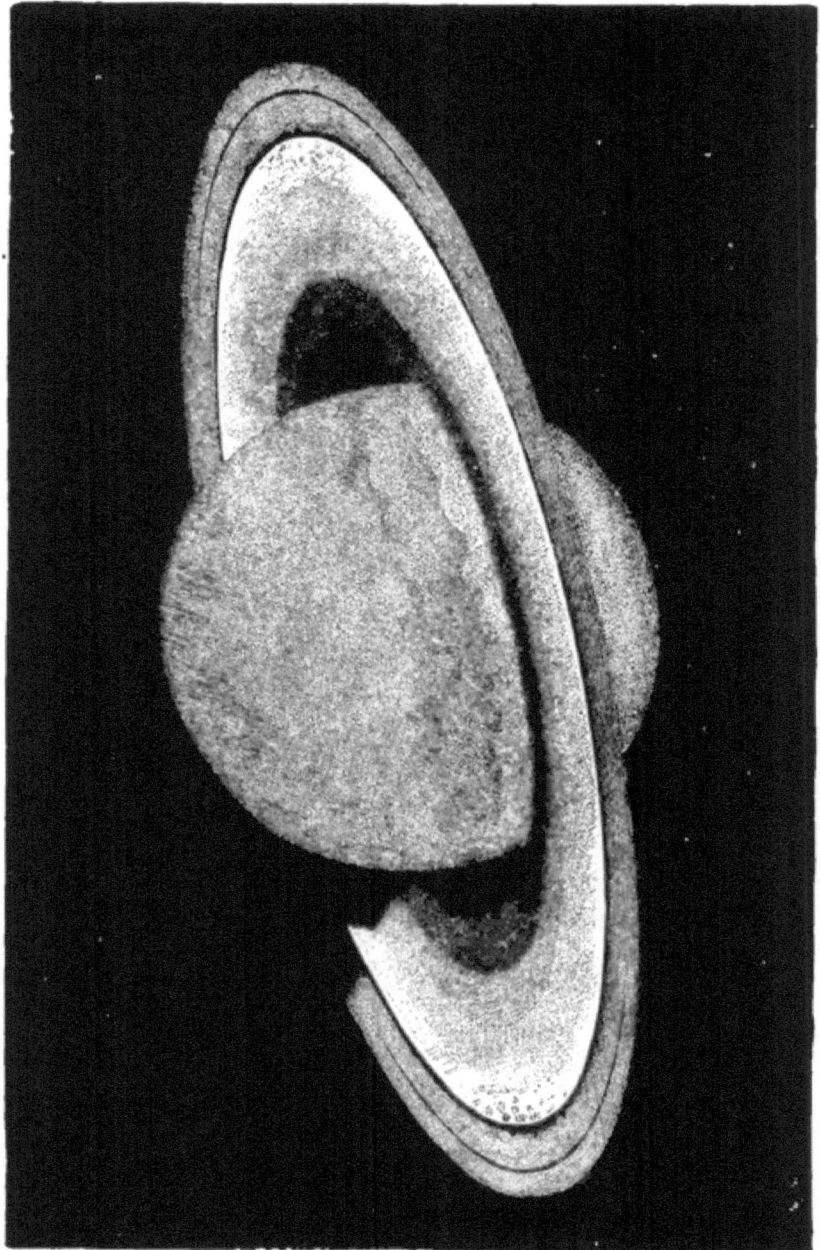

Details of the ring of Saturn observed by Trouvelot with the 26-inch Washington Refractor.

looked at. The eye-piece is the small glass near the eye."

"Is that telescope like the one Galileo invented?" asked Harry.

"It is much more powerful," replied Dr. Willoughby. "The object-glass in Galileo's was about an inch

Saturn and his moons (general view with a 3 3-4-inch object-glass.)

in diameter, and this is eight inches. There is a large telescope in the Washington Observatory, made by Mr. Alvan Clark, that has an object-glass of twenty-six inches. It makes a great difference in looking at the heavenly bodies whether one has a three-inch glass, or one of twenty-six inches."

"I should think it would," said Harry.

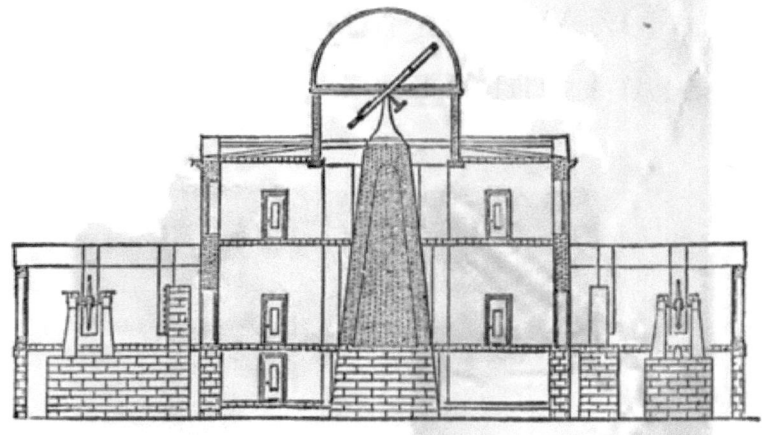

Section of Main Building — United States Naval Observatory, showing support of Equatorial.

"It is important large telescopes should be perfectly steady," continued the Professor, "and in Observatories they are often placed upon solid mason-work, built up from the ground, and not touching the walls or floors

of the building at any point.   One of
the finest telescopes in the United

Cambridge (U. S.) Equatorial, showing Observing Chair and rails.

States is at Cambridge.   The object-
glass is fifteen inches in diameter.

The Obsevatory has a revolving Dome, with an opening in it, which closes with shutters. This Dome turns by machinery, so that the tele-scope can be directed through the opening toward any part of the heav-ens. The chair in which the ob-server sits is made so that it can be easily raised or lowered, and it runs on circular rails round the tele-scope, and so can always be placed in the right position for the ob-server."

"O, how I would like to go there," said Harry.

"Perhaps you will some time," replied the Professor, " and now it is time to go home."

Then they left the cool and shady

Common, and took their way through crowded streets to the station, all agreeing that they had accomplished a great deal, and had a delightful day.

Chapter X.

Astronomy and Fishing.

The next time Professor Willoughby came to Lotus Bay, he found the ladies and children just starting on a fishing excursion with Captain Kidds, Mr. Marlow having gone to drive with another kind neighbor.

Harry eagerly proposed that he should join them, and the others cordially seconding the invitation, he was easily persuaded, and they were soon dancing over the blue waves, with plenty of hooks and lines, and a good supply of bait.

"We're going to catch scup, Doctor Willoughby," said Nelly, "and you must stay to tea, and have some; you can't think how nice they are!"

"Perhaps he's had some at the Pokonoket," suggested Harry.

Nelly looked disappointed, but smiled again when the Professor assured her he had not yet tasted her favorite fish.

"The whole word is *Scuppaug*," said Harry.

"And they're just like silver," cried Nelly, "all over lovely shiny white."

"How far out are you going to take us, Captain?" asked Mrs. Marlow, who was a little timid on the water, and now looked anxiously at the long space between them and the wharf they had just left.

"Only as far as the second buoy, Marm," was the answer, "as long as it's only scup we're after."

They soon reached the buoy, and Captain Kidds having fastened the boat to it, began, with Harry's help, to bait the hooks for the rest. Presently every line was thrown over, and every face assumed an expression of patient expectation. It was a long time before any one had a bite, and Harry soon broke the silence by saying in a low tone to the Professor who sat next him:

"I wonder if we could see that spot on the Sun to-day if we had a telescope."

"Very likely," said the Professor;

" a Sun-spot sometimes lasts several months, and sometimes it vanishes in a few hours. The Sun turns from East to West on its axis in about twenty-six days. We know this because the spots seem to move across the disc in about a fortnight, though it is really the Sun that moves, and carries them with him. The spots are first seen on the Eastern edge; then they appear to pass across to the Western edge, and then they disappear. After about fourteen days they re-appear on the Eastern edge again. This is a little longer than the time it takes the Sun to turn on his axis, because the Earth is all the while moving round the Sun in her path."

Here Nelly caught a scup, and

loudly begged the Professor to ad-
mire its silvery beauty, which he
did, to her entire satisfaction. It
was then dropped into the pail
brought for the purpose, and Dr.
Willoughby resumed his remarks to
Harry.

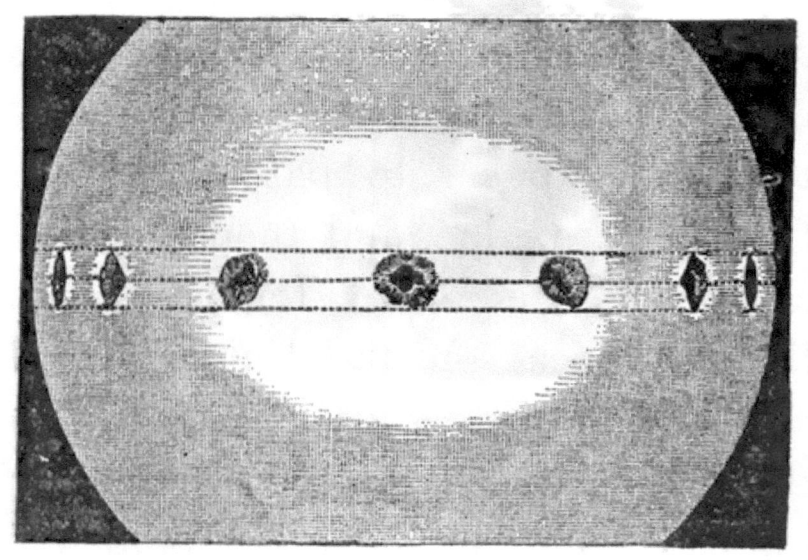

The same spot seen at different points of the Sun.

"As these spots move, or appear
to move across the Sun, they vary in

shape, being larger and broader when on the middle of his disc, and growing narrower as they approach the edge. When a large spot comes to the edge, a notch can sometimes be seen there,

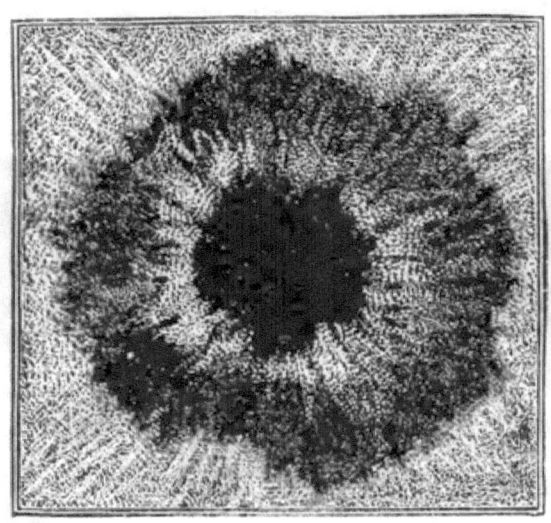

Front view of a spot on the Sun.

showing that the spot is a cavity or opening."

"The man said they were openings in the bright clouds, but what makes them?" asked Harry.

" Sir John Herschel, the astronomer, supposed them to be caused by tornadoes and whirlwinds," replied the Professor.

Spot observed close to the edge of the Sun.

The conversation was now interrupted by Harry and the Doctor's each pulling up a fine scup, after which Miss Roseberry distinguished herself by catching a sculpin, which was thrown back as useless, after Mrs. Marlow had wondered at its big mouth and curious horns.

In the next quiet interval, Harry inquired, "How large are these spots ever seen?"

"Sometimes they are twenty-five thousand miles or more in diameter. There is generally a dark centre; next comes a border of gray clouds, and then bright streaks of light called Faculæ, supposed to be masses of vapor, thousands of miles long. But the Sun is so dazzling, it is difficult to study his surface."

"The telescope must always have a dark glass in it to protect the eye, must it not?" inquired Miss Roseberry, who was near enough to overhear the conversation.

"Yes," replied the Professor; "if you should look at the blazing Sun through a telescope without this colored glass, you would lose your eye-sight."

"I never thought of that," said

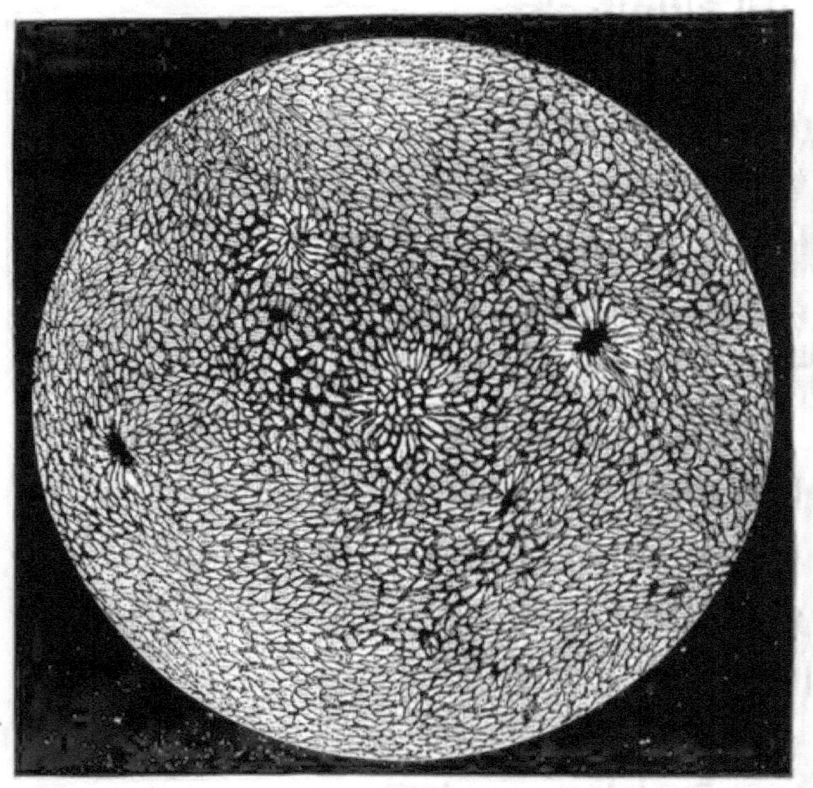

Appearance of the Sun's surface as seen through powerful glasses.

Harry; "isn't it strange when the Sun looks so bright to us, there can be large black spots on it?"

" If we look at it with a powerful telescope," said the Professor, " the surface seems to be mottled or dotted with small, oval grains. These have been called willow-leaves, or rice grains, from their shape. They are thought to be smaller openings in the fleecy clouds, I believe."

"Are there always spots on the Sun ?" asked Harry.

" No," replied his · friend; " they diminish in number during five years or so, and then increase again for about five years. There were a great many in 1870."

Here Harry discovered that his bait had been entirely nibbled off, but after taking a fresh bait, he began to catch scup so fast that he forgot all about the Sun. At the end of two hours it was found that Nelly had caught seven, Harry eleven, the Professor and Mrs. Marlow each five, while Miss Miranda had only two, but was redeemed by Captain Kidds who boasted of fourteen. It was decided that these would make an ample supper, and the Captain accordingly cast off from the buoy and took charge of the rudder, while Harry and Miss Roseberry each grasped an oar and pulled gallantly home.

After tea, when Mrs. Marlow had gone to put Nelly to bed, and Mr. Marlow and the Professor had become absorbed in a political discussion, Miss Roseberry and Harry slipped away to their favorite west door step. Here, bye and bye, the

Professor joined them, and they resumed their talk about the Sun.

" I wish I could see a total eclipse of the Sun," said Miss Roseberry;

Total Eclipse of the Sun, August 7th, 1869, showing the Corona and Prominences.

"the Corona must be so beautiful."
" I thought it was too dark to see

much of anything in a total eclipse," said Harry.

" When the Moon comes between the Sun and the Earth, and acts as

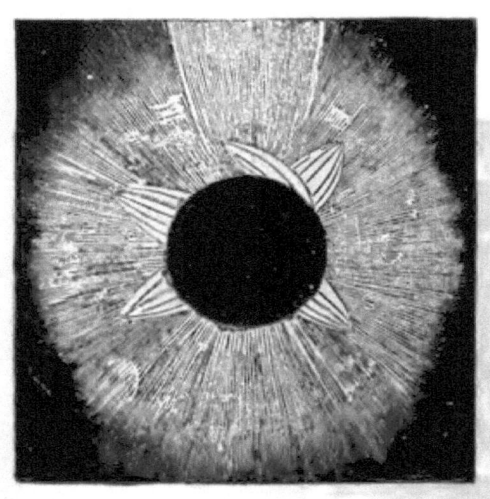

The Eclipse of 1858 (Liais), showing Prominences.

a shade to hide the Sun's brightness," said the Professor, "there can be seen around the dark edge of the Moon, a Corona or Crown of silvery light, rising above the Sun's surface, to a height of two or three hundred

thousand miles, and besides the Corona there are rose-colored flames
which stream out around the edge of
the Moon. These are called the
Red Prominences, and they have

Solar Explosions.

been compared to garnets round a
brooch of jet.

" How perfectly exquisite it must be," said Miss Miranda.

" Are they on the Sun or on the Moon?" asked Harry.

" There was formerly much doubt as to whether they belonged to the Sun, the Moon, or to our atmosphere," replied the Professor, "but they are now supposed to belong to the Sun."

"What are they?" persisted Harry.
" I believe astronomers are still in doubt about the Corona, though it is thought to be caused partly by reflected Sun-light ; but it has been discovered by means of the Spectroscope (which is an instrument composed of two small telescopes, having a prism between them), that the Red Prominences are flames thrown off,

by a mass of hydrogen gas which surrounds the Sun, and is so hot as to shine by its own light. This envelope of gas is called the Chromosphere, and the bright surface of the Sun is called the Photosphere."

Student's Spectroscope.

"How can they find out with a Spectroscope," asked Harry.

"When a sunbeam passes through a prism, a band of rainbow colors is formed which is called the Solar

Spectrum. Haven't you seen it when the Sun strikes the glass drops of a chandelier, Harry ?"

"O, yes, often, and I knew the drops were prisms, but I didn't know what the colors were called," answered Harry.

Illustrating the Dark Lines of the Solar System.

"The white light is really made up of these rainbow colors," continued the Professor, "and the prism separates them. If we let the light of a candle, or the light of burning hydrogen gas, or any bright light pass through a prism, it will be broken or split up in the same way, and the band of colors thus made is called the spectrum of the candle, or the spectrum of the gas, or whatever the light may be. Each kind of light shows a different spectrum. When astronomers let the light from the Red Prominences pass through the prism of the Spectroscope, they recognized the spectrum that belongs to glowing hydrogen, so they knew that the flames must be from hydrogen surrounding the Sun? Am I not tiring you with all this?"

"O, no!" cried Harry and Miss Roseberry, together, "do go on!"

"Very well, then," he resumed, "we know that the Sun shines by its own light, and the ancients called it a globe of fire. It is now thought to be made up of gases and metals, most of which are found upon the

Earth, only, upon the Earth they are solid, while in the Sun the heat is so intense that they are all in the form of vapor. It has been calculated that if the Earth were covered with a layer of ice one hundred feet thick, the heat we receive from the Sun in a year would melt it; and as to the light of the Sun it is equal to more than five thousand wax candles at a distance of one foot from the eye."

"I do wish Abner could hear that," said Harry; "but I suppose he never would believe it."

"Another beautiful appearance connected with the Sun," continued Dr. Willoughby, "is the Zodiacal Light. This is a cone of faint light which stretches up above the horizon at certain seasons. In the winter and spring it may be seen after twilight rising from the western horizon, and in summer and autumn in the east before day-break."

"What is it supposed to be?" asked Miss Roseberry.

"One theory is that it is sunlight reflected from a cloud of little meteors between the Sun and the Earth," said the Professor, "but here comes the boy with my horse, and I must bid you good-night."

"O, come to-morrow and tell us more," cried Harry, clinging to him.

"Shall I?" asked the Professor of Miss Roseberry.

She smiled, and he added: "Then, I will; good-night."

Chapter XI.

LAST DAYS AT LOTUS BAY.

The Professor came early the next afternoon in a two-seated carriage, and invited Miranda and the children to take a drive with him. They were soon ready, and Miss Roseberry and Nelly taking the back seat, and the Professor and Harry the front, they started in good spirits; Nelly remarking that if only Major and the colt were following, she should think they were going to Hackmatack Mountain.

It was not long before Harry resumed the talk of the previous evening by asking the Professor if Meteors were shooting stars.

"Yes," he replied, "Meteor is from a Greek word which means *things in the air.* Have you never seen them flashing through the sky?"

"O, yes," answered Harry; "once when we were sitting on the door-step, we saw a big one go by, didn't we, Cousin Miranda? but it was gone before we had time to look at it."

"They rush along twice as fast as our Earth," said the Professor; "nearly any clear night, one can see four or five in an hour, but about the 10th of August and the 13th of November there are thousands to be seen, and every thirty-three years there is a great star-shower. The

last was in 1866 or 1867. It used
to be supposed that Meteors were
thrown from volcanoes in the Moon,
but astronomers have since concluded
that millions of them are continually
traveling round the Sun, and that
now and then our Earth crosses their
path, and then we see swarms of
them. They fly along so swiftly that
when they come within our atmosphere, they become very hot and
bright, and some of them burn up entirely. Others explode, and the fragments come tumbling down upon the
Earth. These fragments are called
Aerolites, or Bolides, and are composed partly of iron and nickel. Some
have been found weighing more than
a thousand pounds. There is a very
large one in the Smithsonian Insti-

Bolide in fusion observed over Athens.

209

tute in Washington, which fell in Arizona. It is as tall as Nelly, but not very thick, and has a large hole in the middle. It looks like an enormous mass of what is commonly called 'clinker' from a furnace or coal-stove."

"I should be sorry to be near when it fell," said Miss Roseberry.

"Yes," said Dr. Willoughby, "they are often nearly buried in the ground where they strike, so great is the force they have acquired. In old times, people were very much afraid of both Meteors and Comets, but we know too much about them now to consider them omens of coming evils."

"Are there many Comets, too?" asked Harry.

"Many thousands," replied the

Professor, "but most of them can be seen only with a telescope. They usually have a nucleus or head surrounded by a sort of haze called the Coma, and a long train of light streaming from them out over the heavens sometimes millions of miles, and yet so thin that even small stars can be seen through it. Some Comets move round the Sun, in long, oval paths, and seem to belong to him as the Planets do, but others suddenly appear and then vanish, and are never seen again. One Comet was seen to divide into two, which traveled side by side through the sky, and there is another which appears every seventy-five or seventy-six years. It was last seen in 1835, so it will be visible here again in 1911."

" I remember seeing a very beautiful Comet in the autumn of 1858," said Miss Miranda; " it had a magnificent curved tail like a fiery feather. That was Donati's, was it not?"

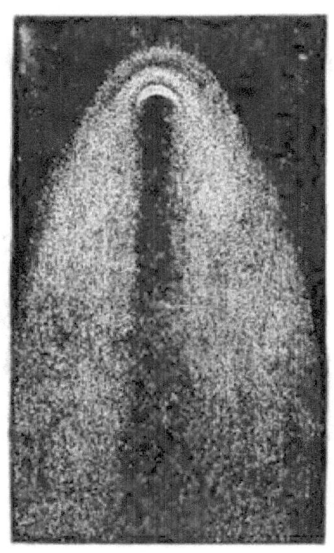

Donati's Comet, 1858.

"Yes," replied the Professor, " it was discovered by Donati, at Florence, and named for him. It was one of the most brilliant ever seen."

"I wish I could see it," cried Harry and Nelly together.

"I am afraid you never will," responded Dr. Willoughby; "for it is supposed to be nearly two thousand years in going round in its path, and you will hardly live to see its next appearance."

At this point Nelly saw some blackberries by the roadside, and begged to be allowed to get out and gather them. So the conversation turned upon other things, and Harry forgot all about astronomy until after tea, when he suddenly inquired:

"Doctor Willoughby, how can you tell which is North?"

"If you have a compass it is very easy," said the Professor.

"Yes, I know about that," said

Harry, "but I mean if you were off in a desert somewhere, and hadn't any compass."

"If you stand with your back to the Sun at noon you will be facing the North, and at night you can tell by the North Star."

"Cousin Miranda showed us how to find the North Star once, Nelly, don't you remember!" said Harry.

"O, yes," said Nelly, "it was a big bear, and he always points to it."

"Why, no it wasn't, Nelly, it was a dipper," said Harry; "two of the stars point to it, but I forget which they are."

"Come out on the doorstep a moment and I'll show you," said the Professor, leading the way. Harry and Nelly followed. "There," he continued, "you see those seven bright stars over Captain Kidds' wood-shed ; four of them form the body of the Dipper, and the other three the handle."

"There, Nelly! I told you it was a dipper," said Harry.

"But the Dipper is part of the constellation or group of stars called Ursa Major, or the Great Bear," added the Professor.

"Aha! I told you it was a bear," said Nelly.

"If you imagine a line drawn from the bottom of the Dipper to the top through the two stars on the side farthest from the handle, and prolong it a little in the same direction, you will reach the North Star."

" Is it that one all by itself ? " said Harry, "and not very large ? "

" Yes," said the Professor, " it is a star of the second magnitude, and is called Polaris. It is at the tip of the Little Bear's tail, or at the end of the handle of the small Dipper. Two of the stars in the Little Bear are quite faint, but the other two you can see plainly enough. The brightest one is called Kochab."

" I see them," said Nelly, " two bright ones, and two little dull ones."

" So do I," said Harry, " but the handle crooks round the wrong way. I like the big Dipper better."

" Those two brighter ones are called the Guardians of the Pole," said Professor Willoughby, "because they always move around it. The Pole, you know, Nelly, is an imaginary point in the heavens, and as the North Star is the nearest bright star to it, they call it the Pole-Star. It is about a degree and a half from the Pole, and moves round it in a small circle."

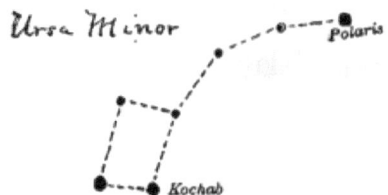

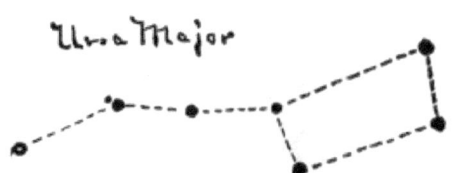

Diagram of Great Bear and Little Bear.

"What did you mean by second magnitude?" asked Harry.

"The stars are arranged in six classes," replied the Professor, "according to their magnitude or size, but this only means their *apparent* size. The brightest may be larger than other stars, or they may only be nearer the Earth. The brightest are called stars of the first magnitude, the next brightest are of the second magnitude, and so on to the sixth class, which are the smallest that can be seen without a telescope. With a telescope a great many more can be seen. If you should watch Ursa Minor, the Little Bear, you would see that he appears to move round the Pole once in twenty-four hours."

"Why do they call it a bear?" asked Harry, "it doesn't look much like one."

" In looking at the sky," replied the Professor, " you notice that all the stars seem to be arranged in groups or clusters. In early times men gave names to these star-groups, or constellations, from some fancied resemblance to animals, such as bears, lions, eagles, &c. In most cases the résemblance is not easily seen, but the old names are kept to prevent confusion, and it is necessary to know them, because they are used in books of astronomy."

" I have sometimes thought," said Miss Roseberry, " that when less was known of the art of drawing, men might have been more easily satisfied by a rude resemblance."

" I like to have them called bears

and lions," said Nelly; "it's a great deal more interesting than just stars and planets, and I can remember them better, too."

"Many of the constellations are connected with old fables of the Gods and Greek heroes," continued Dr. Willoughby; "you'd like that, Nelly."

"O, yes!" cried the little girl, "do tell us the story about the Great Bear."

"According to the Greek fable," said the Professor, "that was once a beautiful princess, named Callisto, with whom Juno became so angry that she turned her into a bear. When the poor Princess found her pretty hands turning into heavy paws, and her nails into pointed claws, she cried to Jupiter for help, but as her voice was now only a hoarse growl, he did not hear her."

"O, dear!" cried Nelly, looking at her own chubby fingers, "how she must have felt when she saw them all black and ugly!"

"As she was now a bear," resumed the Professor, "she was obliged to live in the woods. One day she was startled by a hunter, and as she turned to fly from him, she saw it was her own son, Arcas. Of course he did not recognize her, and would have killed her, but Jupiter at last came to the rescue, and saved both by snatching them up into the heavens and placing them among the stars."

"O, that was good," sighed Nelly,

and would have asked for a second story, but here Mrs. Marlow called to her to come in and go to bed. Harry, who thought the fables rather foolish, was not sorry to have his turn, and at once inquired, " How many stars are there in all ? "

" There are more than three thousand visible without a glass," replied his friend, " and many more to be seen with one. In early times men watched them carefully, studying their rising and setting and their motions across the sky. Travelers in the desert and on the sea were guided by them, particularly by the Pole-Star, as that is always in nearly the same place. It is said the Phœnician sailors steered by Ursa

Minor and the Greeks by Ursa Major."

> " Seven equal stars adorn the greater Bear,
> And teach the Grecian sailors how to steer,"

quoted Miss Roseberry.

" Thank you," said the Professor, " you must remember that, Harry."

" I wonder how Capt. Kidds would feel if he had only the Bear to go by," said Harry. " Those old sailors must have had hard times when it was cloudy at night, and they had no light-houses. Is the Great Bear always in the North, Dr. Willoughby ? "

" Yes, it moves around the North Pole once every twenty-four hours, and is seen sometimes on the right, and sometimes on the left of the

North-Star; sometimes near the horizon, sometimes far above it, but always in the North."

"It is the same as 'Charles's Wain,' is it not?" asked Miss Roseberry.

"The seven stars that form the Dipper are sometimes called Charles's Wain, or wagon," replied the Professor, "because they look a little like a wagon drawn by three horses in a line."

"Somewhat as we looked, going in Abner's wagon, with the old horse and the colt, and Major," laughed Harry.

"The Arabs had still another fancy," added Dr. Willoughby; "they compared it to a bier with mourners, and called the star at the tip of the tail, Benetnasch, or chief, as it stood in the place of the head-mourner, the four stars forming the bier."

"What are the pointers named?" asked Harry.

"The one nearest the Pole is Dubhe, and the other Merak. The middle one is Mizar, and that has a small companion star named Alcor, which the Arabians called *the proof*, as it was considered a proof of good eye-sight to see it. Just now it is a little below Mizar."

"I see it!" cried Harry, "so my eyes are good."

"So can I," said Miranda, "but I am most pleased that you can, Professor Willoughby, for it proves that your sight is really improving."

"You are kind to remember that,"

he answered, much pleased. " Yes, I am glad to say my eyes are almost as well as ever, though I am advised to rest them a few months longer. To return to sailors," he resumed after a pause, " instead of having only the stars to guide them, they now have the Compass, the Chronometer, and the Nautical Almanac, and many other guides."

" I saw a Nautical Almanac at Captain Kidds, to-day," said Harry. " It was full of figures ; I couldn't understand much except what it told about light-houses, and when the tide will be high in different places."

" It is invaluable to seamen," said the Professor, " it helps them find their way across the pathless ocean; it gives the time when the Moon will pass the principal stars that are near her path, and her distance from these stars during every day in the year. It foretells Eclipses, and contains much more information about the Sun and the Planets, which enables them to determine accurately their latitude and longitude, or in other words, to find out as exactly where they are, as if they could see a map of the world, with their own ship distinctly marked upon it. You will study all this some time, when you are older, and when Doctor Bonney says you are well enough. The Nautical Almanac is always prepared several years in advance, so that it may be useful to those who make long voyages and cannot go and buy a new one every year.

The one for 1880 was published in 1876."

" How interesting it is," said Miss Roseberry, " to imagine these astronomers toiling at home and tasking their brains day after day, to prepare guides for men they never see, through dangers they themselves perhaps never encounter, each doing what the other could not possibly do, and both equally necessary to the progress of the world."

" Certainly," said the Professor, laughing, "we can fancy Jack Tar saying to Dr. Star : ' you make me an almanac, and I'll go and bring you tea and coffee to keep you awake while you do it ; you regulate my chronometer, and I'll fetch the mahogany for its box.' "

"Captain Kidds has a chrono-meter, too," said Harry, rather sur-prised at these jests, "and it was in a strong, square box, and made so that it kept level all the time, no matter how much the ship pitched about. It is the same as a big watch, isn't it?"

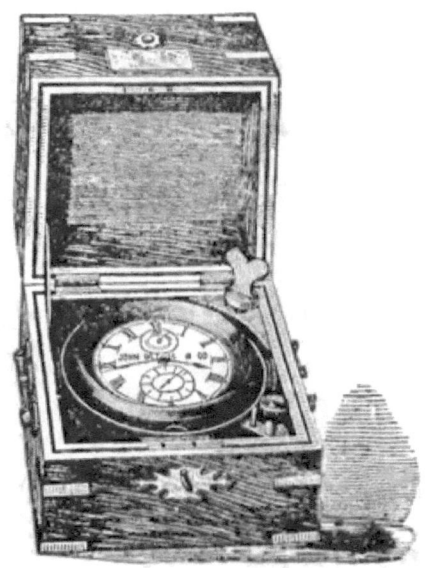

Chronometer.

"Yes," said Dr. Willoughby, "only

that is a more perfect time-keeper, as near perfection as one can be made. Before a captain starts on a voyage, he has his chronometer carefully regulated and put in order by some scientific person."

"Why is he so particular about it?" asked Harry.

"He finds his longitude by it," the Professor answered; "let me see if I can explain it in a few words. As the Earth turns round toward the East, any place east of this town, for example, will have later time than we have, because the motion of the Earth will carry it under the Sun sooner. Fifteen degrees of longitude are equal to one hour of time, that is, fifteen degrees, or about one thousand and fifty miles of the

Earth's surface pass under the Sun in one hour. When it is sunrise here, it will be an hour *after* sunrise at a place fifteen degrees east of us, and it will be an hour *before* sunrise at a place fifteen degrees west of us."

"Then if the Sun rises here at six o'clock, it would be seven o'clock fifteen degrees east of us, and five o'clock at the same distance westward?" said Miss Roseberry.

"Yes," said the Professor. "When the Sun is on the Meridian, it is twelve o'clock."

"What is the Meridian?" said Harry.

"It is an imaginary line drawn from the North to the South point of the horizon through the zenith.

Chronometers are generally set by Greenwich time, and they reckon longitude from the Meridian which passes through that place. You know it is near London, and there is a famous observatory. When the captain sees the Sun on the Meridian at twelve o'clock, you know, he looks at his chronometer; suppose now he should find it to be one o'clock by this chronometer; then allowing fifteen degrees to an hour, he would know that he was fifteen degrees west of Greenwich. Or, if the chronometer time was three o'clock, he would know that he was forty-five degrees west. But if the chronometer said eleven o'clock, when the Sun said twelve, he would know that he was fifteen degrees *east* of Greenwich, or in longitude fifteen degrees east."

"I think I understand it," said Harry, but his voice sounded rather tired, and the Professor soon after bade them all good-night, and returned to his hotel!"

CHAPTER XII.

AUTUMN CHANGES.

Two days after this Harry came hurrying in from a walk to the post-office, looking quite excited.

"Where's Cousin Miranda?" he asked of Nelly, who was sitting on the door-step, with her six dolls.

"Up-stairs," said Nelly.

"I've brought her a letter," said Harry, "and while I take it up I wish you'd go and tell father there's no mail for him to-day," and he disappeared up the stairs, as Nelly carefully set Miss Cecelia Willoughby Estella Marlow in a leaning position against the scraper, and went to do his errand, with a patient little sigh over the interruption to her many cares. Harry found his cousin reading " The Cruise of the Betsey," a book Dr. Willoughby had lent her, but she laid it in her lap with a smile, when she saw him coming with a letter.

" It's the Professor's handwriting," began the boy in an injured tone. " I don't see what he wants to write to you for, instead of to me! May I wait, and hear what he says about coming ?"

" Certainly," said Miss Roseberry; looking quite flushed and excited, too, but stopping to study the address and seal so long, that Harry felt very impatient. " You seldom see

a seal now-a-days" she remarked.
" Look, Harry, what a nice, clear
W it is!" and she carefully cut off
the end of the envelope with her
scissors, instead of breaking the wax.
Then at last she took out the letter,
and poor Harry felt more jealous
than ever when he saw there were
two well-filled sheets. Dr. Willoughby
had never written so much to him.
He walked to the window and leaned
half out with his back to his cousin,
to pretend he didn't care, and re-
lieved his mind by picking off ripe
morning-glory seeds, and sprinkling
them down upon Nelly and her
family.

Presently he heard Miss Roseberry
say : " O, Harry !" and he turned

quickly to see what made her voice sound so strange.

"Just think!" she said, half reading, and half repeating from the letter; "he found a note from Mrs. Parsnips when he went home that night, and she says that Abner is very sick with rheumatic fever, and everything is going wrong on the farm, and she wants the Professor to come back and help her; and he's gone; and he don't know when he can see us again, but he'll write and let us know soon how Abner is. Poor Mrs. Parsnips! Isn't it too bad?"

"I should think you'd say poor Abner," said Harry. "Yes, it *is* too bad; but go on. What else? You

haven't read half, I'm sure. Abner
isn't dead, is he?"

"O, no, indeed!" replied his
cousin. "I've read you every word
there is about Hickory Corners,"—
(here to Harry's surprise and dis-
gust, she quietly folded up the letter and put it in her pocket) "and
don't you want to go and tell Nelly
about it?"

Harry knew he was dismissed, and
he went slowly down-stairs, feeling
very unhappy.

"I never thought Cousin Miranda
would be so mean," he said to himself. "I should think it was bad
enough to have *my* Dr. Willoughby
snatched away to New Hampshire,
and no knowing when I shall see
him again; and there's Abner to feel

sorry about, too,—and now she won't even let me see his letter! I showed her both of mine, right off!"

By this time, Harry had reached Nelly, and I fear he took a cruel pleasure in telling her that Abner was very sick indeed, would possibly die, and that then of course Dr. Willoughby would have to stay with Mrs. Parsnips, and perhaps never come to see them any more. By the time the tears began to run down tender-hearted Nelly's cheeks, Harry's bad temper was half over, and just as he was soothing her by suggesting that perhaps Abner was better by this time, and maybe there'd be another letter from the Professor to-morrow, his cheerfulness was entirely restored by the appearance of two tall, manly-looking boys who were coming along the road, and who called out to know if he wouldn't like to go fishing with them.

"Yes! Yes! Wait a minute!" he cried, and rushing into the parlor, exclaimed:

"O, mamma! Hal Carleton and Dick Rodgers are going fishing, and want me to go too. Say, quick, can I?"

"Yes," said Mrs. Marlow, "I am always willing you should go with them, only get Mary to put you up some luncheon, and be sure and get home before dark."

"All right!" said Harry, and went away quite happy again. Nelly, however, was left rather lonely, especially as Cousin Miranda remained in her

own room all the forenoon, and after
dinner, instead of taking the little
girl to walk, as she generally did,
slipped away alone toward the shore,
and did not return till nearly tea-
time. And even after tea, instead
of coming out on the door-step to
join the young people in a game of
" Twenty Questions," or " Throwing
Light " (for Hal and Dick had come
over) as she always had before, she
was shut up with Mrs. Marlow, talking, till the visitors went away, and
Nelly had to go to bed.

Both the children thought Cousin
Miranda seemed rather queer, but in
the course of the next day everything
was explained and forgiven by their
mother's confiding to them as a great
secret that Dr. Willoughby had asked

Miranda to be his wife, and that she had promised that she would.

The children were so surprised and bewildered that for a moment they gazed at their mother with wide open eyes, in silence.

"Oho!" said Harry, "that was why she wouldn't show me that letter, I suppose, and why she went to the Post Office herself this morning."

"Perhaps so," said Mrs. Marlow. "I don't know; but, remember not to tease her, and not to speak of it to any one but your father and me."

Then she went into the house, leaving Harry and Nelly in the barn, where they were arranging their scallop shells.

" Do you suppose we shall have to call her Mrs. Willoughby now ? " asked Nelly, after a while.

" *I* shan't," said Harry, " I shall say Cousin Miranda just the same, and I shouldn't wonder if by and by we called him Cousin John."

" O, how funny that would be," said Nelly, " and of course there'll be a wedding like Cousin George's, and we shall be invited. I shall like that. I should like to have a pink dress."

" I don't care for weddings," said Harry, " but I tell you what *will* be good fun. If they invite us to ——, where his college is, next summer. There must be a telescope there."

All these pleasant anticipations

were fully realized, even to the pink dress.

Abner soon grew better, and by the time the Marlow family returned to Boston, the Professor could be spared from Hickory Corners, and was often at their house.

As his eyes were not to be tasked for several months, he persuaded Miss Roseberry that an early marriage, and a winter spent in seeing Washington and Florida would be the best preparation for resuming his college duties in the spring, and when this was all settled, he farther proposed, that as Doctor Bonney still forbade Harry's going to school, the boy should go with them. Nelly shed a few tears, but was consoled by being promised a letter every fortnight, with her own name on it, and having her dear friend Milly Hoffman take tea with her every Saturday.

Harry himself was as happy as the Professor, which is saying much, and was overheard by his mother remarking to Nelly:

"I think it's quite proper I should go, for you know if it hadn't been for my talking to him in the cars, Cousin Miranda might never have known him."

"Then I ought to go too," said Nelly, "for if I hadn't fallen out of the carriage, he couldn't have caught me, and that was really the first of it."

"Not at all," interrupted Mrs. Marlow, "it was my asking Cousin

Miranda to go with you to Hickory Corners."

" And who recommended Hickory Corners ? " said Dr. Bonney, coming up behind them ; for this was at the wedding, and all the friends were there.

" The only way to settle it," said Mr. Marlow, " is to say, it was written *in the Stars.*"

THE END.

www.ingramcontent.com/pod-product-compliance
Lightning Source LLC
Chambersburg PA
CBHW030808020726
47499CB00006B/1823